Carol DeChant

ARE YOU FREE?

Till Death Do Us Part?

AUSTIN MACAULEY PUBLISHERS™
LONDON • CAMBRIDGE • NEW YORK • SHARJAH

Ordering Information
Quantity sales: Special discounts are available on quantity purchases by corporations, associations, and others. For details, contact the publisher at the address below.

Publisher's Cataloguing-in-Publication data
DeChant, Carol
Are You Free?

ISBN 9798889104827 (Paperback)
ISBN 9798889104834 (Audiobook)
ISBN 9798889104841 (ePub e-book)

Library of Congress Control Number: 2024902452

www.austinmacauley.com/us

First Published 2024
Austin Macauley Publishers LLC
40 Wall Street, 33rd Floor, Suite 3302
New York, NY 10005
USA

mail-usa@austinmacauley.com
+1 (646) 5125767

Table of Contents

1

Faith Without Religion/2008

For the first time in twenty-some years, Dante Moretti needs to go to Confession.

Picking up his car keys, he checks the weather on his cell phone: Sarasota, sunny 74; Laconia, NH, sleet and 14 below. Comparing local weather to where you used to live never gets old, even after decades of "shoveling sunshine," he likes to say. Backing out of the driveway, he heads toward St. Pete and a church he's never been to—hopefully, no one there will recognize the license plate on his Ace-red Porsche: ACE HDW. Dante and his brother, Nick, own thirteen Ace Hardware stores in the bay area.

Dante's a Cafeteria Catholic—choosing for himself from what the Vatican dictates to accept or reject, especially "pelvic issue" ones such as birth control or gay marriage. His daughters Joan and Cecilia, at twenty-three and twenty-one, would call his need for Confession but not for church "faith without religion." Dante would think that inaccurate but can't explain how. Or how even an infrequently observant Catholic still wants Confession. This morning, Dante both yearns for and dreads it.

Light streams through the stained-glass windows, and Dante sits in a pew for a minute to gather his thoughts about how his sister-in-law Rosemary triggered this mess. Rosemary is a screamer—creating scenes in public. Often her position is unfair, against the rules, nutty. Nick and Rosemary were high-school sweethearts, so Dante's observed her for a long time. She seems to harbor an emotional time bomb that builds pressure and must explode every now and then.

This last episode was at the indie film theater after someone complained that Rosemary was talking on her cell. When an usher came to point out that they'd just shown the notice to turn off phones, she argued that trailers were showing so it didn't matter.

Arguing loudly even as she was stowing her phone, Rosemary dropped a bag of sandwiches she'd brought in. Outside food is taboo there. Ultimately, the usher and a manager escorted Rosemary, Nick, Dante, and his date out of the theater. Other theatergoers applauded their leaving. *I should have let it end there*, he thinks, getting up to confess.

The old dark confessional is closed. An arrow points to a door with a sign, "Father Bede." He opens the door and sees a thin, dark-skinned confessor sitting in a well-lit room, smiling. *Third world priest*, Dante thinks. *Mom says that a fourth of the priests in America are recruited from Africa.*

Unsure of the procedure now, he offers a handshake. The priest obviously hadn't expected that—but grasps

Dante's hand with both of his and says, "Sit down, bruddah."

Dante finds brightly lit eyeball-to-eyeball Confession awkward, but with the priest looking at him expectantly, Dante says, "Bless me, Father, for I have sinned. It's been—I don't know—twenty years or more since my last confession."

"What brings you here tuhday?"

"I…gossiped."

"I do not know that whud."

"It's when you tell harmful things about another person."

"A sin of the tongue?"

"Yes."

"Was what you said true?"

"Yes."

"Did you take money for sayin' this?"

"No."

"Where was the harm?"

Conveying what he did after Rosemary's tantrum is way more difficult than Dante had anticipated.

As she does every Thursday, Joan had come over that evening to watch The Apprentice with Dante and Cecilia. That night, she came early, having heard from her Uncle Nick that the older generation got kicked out of the movie. Joan opened the pizza on a coffee table in front of the TV. Eager to get the story, she asked, "Was that a menopause meltdown Aunt Rosemary had the other night at the movie?"

"No, just one of your aunt's outbursts. As your Nani has said, 'Rosemary is *highly strung*'."

"*Highly strung?* Aunt Rosie's not a *violin*. She's screaming ME! ME! ME! She turns every special event into a focus on herself. Poor Uncle Nick. How can he put up with her?"

"Rosemary has many good qualities. And she's family," Dante says, the Parent.

Cecilia asks, "Has Uncle Nick ever…?" raising an eyebrow to indicate playing around. The girls giggle.

"Don't go there," Dante says. But he's laughing too, and they notice.

"He has! Tell us!" Joan snorts when she laughs.

"No. It was nothing, a long time ago, very brief." Dante, Loyal Brother.

"OK, good. So it's history. Then just tell us when," Cecilia says, the Negotiator.

"You were just kids," Dante says, weakening. "Do you recall when Uncle Nick and Aunt Rosemary renewed their vows?"

"I never understood that: do wedding vows expire?" Cecilia asks, extending her arm as a trail of mozzarella stretches from a pizza slice to her mouth.

Then Joan says, "Wasn't that an unusual anniversary year? Eighteen? Sixteen? And wasn't Aunt Rosemary wearing a formal bridal gown to renew their vows?"

"Yes, yes. Rosemary lost a lot of weight, and they hadn't originally had a formal wedding. I guess she wanted to put her new slim figure into a wedding dress and have a big ceremony."

"So bizarre," says Joan.

"You think?" Cecilia says. "But what does this have to do with Uncle Nick's…dalliance?"

Temptation triumphs; it's such a good story. "A gal named Kate O'Malley catered the party they had after the vow renewal," Dante said. "It was that Irish girl."

Cecilia shrieks, "Their caterer for the wedding vow renewal?"

Joan leans back on the sofa, laughing: "How did this happen?"

"Well, Rosemary was dieting, so she sent Nick to sample cake choices. The Irish girl's company's called "Katering—spelled with a K—& Events." When he got there, she was busy with another client, so he sat, waiting. She was rushing to her kitchen and back but welcomed Nick and asked if she could help him. He knew she was still busy with the other customer so—you know Uncle Nick: not wanting to impose—he says, 'Are you free?' And she says, 'I'm not *free*, but I'm *very* reasonable.' Obviously flirting."

His daughters lean against one another, laughing. "How long did it last?" Joan, blotting her eyes.

"Not long. It isn't in Nick's nature to cheat," Dante says. "And maybe the Irish girl had other… clients." They all laugh.

Dante's merriment is short-lived. After the pizza, Cecilia goes upstairs to bed, and Joan takes the pizza boxes home to hide the evidence of their dinner from Nani. Dante thinks of all the cooked dinners Rosemary brought to them after the shock of his wife Lilliana's death. Rosemary knew that Cecilia had just got her first period right before that—the worst time to be without a mother. Rosie called her mother-in-law, Dante and Nick's mother, to come from Laconia to stay with them for a while. That was eight years ago, and Mom-Angelina-Nani has stayed.

Angelina forbids restaurant pizza, but they like those from the wood-burning trattoria, so they order them Thursdays—when Angelina goes to Franny's house to bake biscotti for Italian weddings and funerals at the parish. She stays overnight with Franny rather than drive back late. After Joan leaves with the pizza boxes and leftovers, Dante goes to the patio to light a cigarette. The three women in his life believe he quit smoking. *Lots of duplicities here*, he thinks, as the white cloud of smoke mixes with a black cloud of guilt to engulf him.

"The harm was to my brother. I betrayed his confidence by telling something he'd confided to me," Dante tells Father Bede.

"Why did you do that?"

Dante winces. "To entertain my daughters. Tell a good story, make them laugh."

"Ah, the glamour of evil," the priest says. "Is there anything else?"

"Well, I looked up the Ten Commandments to remind myself, and I didn't really get beyond the first one."

"Idolatry."

"Yes, putting 'false gods' first. Putting the wrong things front and center. Laziness. I haven't gone to Mass, except for Christmas and Easter in all these years. Then, cigarettes, which lead me to lie to my family that I've quit smoking."

"And leads to harming your body."

"Yes. And, while we're on that, gluttony. Bad unrestrained fast-food mornings and afternoons—not taking the time to eat properly and *that* mostly due to impatience during everyday work exchanges or phone calls. My time is more important than whoever's taking it, needlessly. Though it isn't needless to them. I'm blessed in many ways, and aware of it. But I envy people—men—in a good marriage. I had it once, and I'm widowed now."

"Do you wish ill of these happily married men?"

"No. Oh, no. I just wish…I had that."

"It is not sinful to mourn, my friend."

"Well, that brings me to lust, which seems to be a constant condition." Dante's silence is meant to signal that he's done.

"Let us pray," the priest says. Dante recites the Act of Contrition that he learned as a child. The priest seems to be muttering something else in accompaniment.

"For your penance, you are to read the Sermon on the Mount. In the Gospel of Matthew."

Dante waits.

"… and you are to do a good deed. Go now with the peace of Christ."

Is that it? Dante wonders, quietly. *Must be.* He rises and walks out.

Driving back, Dante is stunned. Mom told him the immigrant priests are here because America's Catholic seminary enrollment has shrunk drastically. The immigrants have to adjust to the shock of living amid so much prosperity and information. Mom wonders if the African priests—rightly—see us as "mission territory." This one has been a surprise. And a puzzle.

Dante had expected a penance of prayer that could have kept him in church until sundown. Dante recalls the Bible at home by Mom's chair. She's been in a Bible study group for years, so she has lots of materials. This may be interesting. Still, this penance seems…insubstantial. *Not fitting my decades of bad deeds. What kind of good deed does this unusual priest have in mind?*

###

After his penitent leaves, Father Bede sits, face uplifted, his eyes closed. The *first confession I've heard here of misuse of that organ between the lips. American men focus on that organ between the legs—confessing adultery. Yet to curse or to speak wrongly to destroy another's reputation has not been confessed by an American until now and is surely equally common.*

The priest breathes in and out, in, out. *Hearing a sincere person scrutinize his life is one of the mysterious ways God teaches me.* He smiles, thinking of this man's capability to appreciate the scripture he's about to dwell in. Blessed are those who mourn, for they shall be comforted.

###

On the drive home, Dante recalls being thrown out of that movie theater. *My second date with Lorraine, who'd looked forward to seeing* Slumdog Millionaire*. But I don't* *see enough potential with her to try to explain or atone for Rosemary.* After turning fifty, Dante realized he has more years behind him than ahead. His renewed sense of time as a diminishing resource leads him to often recall what he had, what he'd lost, what's left, and how to spend the time left. *The girls are pushing me to try online dating. I won't find anyone like Lilliana on a freaking dating app.* Approaching an intersection, Dante spots one of Sarasota's new red-light cameras above: *warning me not to move on through the intersection on yellow.* He stops. *But I usually give in to the girls. Well, how bad could it be?*

2

The Helpful Ace Hardware Man/March 2009

Dante gets out the exercise shorts, slips on a faded black and gold Pirates T-shirt, and takes the yoga mat Cecilia bought him out of the drawer on the side of the giant coffee table—a solid yard square of dark walnut that Mom brought from "up north," which dominates the room. He rolls the yoga mat onto the floor next to what furniture merchants in the '70s called the table's Paul Bunyan legs. *Way bigger legs than mine*, he thinks, reaching up to get the TV control off the table and click on CNN.

Orthopedic guy says every pound on my body is like four pounds on my knees, great motivation to do my PT homework. His New Year's resolution was to stop eating any food dispensed from a window into a car. He's replaced his morning Starbucks with plain black coffee at home. Money saved goes to All Faiths Food Bank—another feel-good aspect.

Starting with hamstring sets for each leg, Dante watches the report on Bernie Madoff's scheme. John Roberts reports hundreds of billions of dollars; tens of thousands of victims.

Stretching out on his back for isometric flexion, Dante pushes against his bent knees. CNN lists prominent victims, New Yorkers, Hollywood. Spielberg, Kevin Bacon, and his wife—that Closer gal. Even CNN: Piers Morgan and Larry King. The worst one wiped out—Elie Weisel and his wife, along with their charitable foundation.

Rolling over face down for the prone knee flexion, Dante's riled at that "Ponzi Scheme" label. *Somehow, every financial scam artist ends up giving us Italians a bad name, even a hundred years later.*

When finished, Dante gets up, puts on sunglasses and a hat to protect his bald head, then goes out through the garage. The whistling sound of mourning doves leaving their nest in the oak tree gets his attention. He walks around the house to check the new bird feeder, which supposedly prevents squirrel raids by shutting down access to the seeds when the weight of a squirrel lands on it. The feeder is still pretty full. Experience leaves him reluctant to hope this bird house will not feed squirrels, but his tendency toward hospitality has long been with the mourning doves.

In the front yard, he loves how comfortably his large 6'4" frame slides into the seat of his Ariens Zero Turn riding mower. The morning fog has burnt off, leaving droplets of water on the lawn. He makes wide swaths with the mower, and the fresh wet-grass smell makes him think of balsamic vinegar over sliced cucumbers.

He thinks of Cecilia, now moving back home after breaking up with the bartender. Good riddance—he would have played around. *I need to talk with her about using this new rent-free situation as a springboard to find a real job.* It was a happy day when he lent Joan the purchase price of her own Ace store—now the third generation of Ace owners, starting with the two that Mom and Pop ran in Laconia. Joan's doing well, repays promptly.

Joan and Nick and me in Hardware; Cecilia in software. Creating websites for Republicans. Mom told us as kids of her first vote at twenty-one: JFK. Glad Mom respects that we don't talk politics at home. It's Cecilia's "work," but she's a volunteer. Will she be able to turn her talents into paid work? She needs to—for her own self-esteem.

"Lilliana: We vowed not to raise Trust Fund Kids, and I'm trying my best." Dante lifts his eyes with his vow to Lili's spirit.

Turning the mower, he sees a green SUV pulling over to the curb. A hefty woman—wearing Pepto-Bismol pink nurse scrubs—gets out to look at a tire. She's dismayed.

He drives his mower toward the SUV. When he arrives, she's back in the front seat, talking to an elderly woman in the back. He shuts off the mower, then carefully steps down to land on his "good knee'"leg, and walks toward them. *She's that woman's caregiver.*

He taps on the driver's window, which she rolls down. "Looks like you've got a flat. I saw you from my mower." He points toward his house to allay the women's possible fears over being approached by a large stranger. "I'm Dante" (withholding "Moretti," as last names ending with a vowel can seem threatening to some people). "Can I help? Do you have a spare?" he asks.

"Yayz!" the anxious driver says, obviously relieved. "I vas taking my client to a doctor."

Eastern European, Dante thinks. "It shouldn't take long. I'll get chairs for you. Can you open the trunk?"

"Thank you," the elderly lady in the back leans forward to say, revealing the hump on her back.

"We were absolutely beside ourselves. You're our Good Samaritan." The skin on her hands grabbing the front seat looks tissue-paper thin.

"No worries, ma'am. I'll be right back," Dante says, then heads to the garage.

He returns with two lawn chairs, gets the women seated in the shade, and goes to work. He's done in ten minutes. The ladies' thanks are profuse. He reaches through the window to give each woman several of his ACE business cards listing store locations, knowing they'll be telling this story the rest of the day. Starting at the doctor's office.

"Take care now," he says, waving, as they pull away. Dante knows he is, by his very nature, "Ace's Helpful Hardware Man." The firm's helpfulness culture appeals to him, and he takes pride in being a part of one of America's oldest companies.

Watching the car drive away safely, he knows this was a good deed he would have done anyway. So it's not penance. Plus, the Good Samaritan didn't hand out business cards. Once again, he wonders, *What did that Father Bede have in mind? How will I find what qualifies as absolution to satisfy my strange penance?*

3

Free Radicals/May 2011

Luella Cohen, nutrition counselor, wants to go home, walk Henry, have a glass of chardonnay, and read *Fifty Shades of Grey*. Instead, she has to keep this last appointment with Joan Moretti. Google tells her that Joan owns one of the local Ace Hardware stores, which the Ace Corporate website says means an average annual gross revenue of $2 million. Looking at her own forms, Luella notes that this wealthy woman is age twenty-six, 6'2", 210 pounds, BMI of 27.

"Hello, Joan. Please come in," she says with forced cheer.

"How's it going?" Joan runs her hand through her curly auburn hair, her outstanding feature. Wondering if it's the most natural-looking dye job ever, Luella had googled "red-headed Italians" and found portraits of ancient red-headed Sicilians, starting with Galileo. Red hair was linked with demon possession then, she learned.

Joan walks over to the small round table, where Luella sits, and takes the client's chair. She slides her diary across to Luella who notices that Joan's recorded her weight as 192. No way has she been following the program.

"It's hard to keep motivated. I'm not seeing results," Joan says.

"Let's take a look," says Luella, scanning the eating diary for Week Two of the South Beach Diet's 'bad carbs & sugar detox'. Luella notes that each meal of the entire week is written with the same pen, neatly, line by line. *This was written all at once before our appointment. She's cheating.*

"You've had no alcoholic drinks—or fruit juice?" Luella asks, suspecting the former.

"Not really," Joan sits with the fingers of one hand spread over her neck, where the V of her white shirt opens.

It was a yes-no question, thinks Luella.

"Do other members of your family struggle with weight issues?" Luella asks.

"Dad's a big guy, overweight. I'm very tall but have been OK with weight. I just started putting on weight last year. I've always been daddy's girl, but I'm afraid I'll get to resemble him physically. Men can look better overweight than women can. It doesn't prevent guys from dating, finding someone special. My sister's normal weight, as was my mother, who died when I was fifteen."

"Oh, I'm so sorry. Had it been a long illness?" Luella wonders: *diabetes? cancer?*

"No, she was about to cross a street, and her phone rang, and she was flipping it open, without seeing the car making a right-hand turn into her path."

"How terrible for you so young—and your family. I'm so sorry. Please go on."

"Our family's big weight-loss story was my aunt's, though she's not a blood relative. My family tells her dieting story endlessly."

"What happened?"

"Years ago, she lost forty-some pounds to get back to her high-school graduation weight."

"Going back to high-school weight in middle age isn't usually a realistic goal," Luella says.

"It was to renew their marriage vows. She even wore a bridal gown."

Luella cocks one eyebrow—permission to smile?—Granted.

"They were planning a luncheon after the ceremony," Joan says. "She'd sent my uncle to sample desserts as she was counting calories. This caterer was running back and forth to her kitchen and greeted Uncle Nick."

"He asked this busy caterer 'Are you free?' 'You know, there's no such thing as a free lunch', the caterer said, more or less flirting. He got involved but only for a short time. His wife eventually began seeing someone else—her personal trainer. She divorced Uncle Nick, married the personal trainer, and then gained back all she'd lost and more."

We're getting way off track here, Luella thinks. "That's yo-yo dieting; your aunt probably had what we call starvation reflex from her sharp weight loss. She unleashed a free radical nightmare. That's why we're trying to set healthy lifelong habits of well-being." Luella spreads out Joan's eating diary. "Let's go over your week."

The pages look like a playbook for healthy eating. Lean meats. No fruits. "Did you really eat all these vegetables?" Luella asks.

"I try to," Joan says, hand to throat.

"No ice cream? No pasta?"

"No." Joan's fingers spread across her throat. *Aha,* thinks Luella. *Her tell. Hand at the throat when she lies.*

"I try to avoid asking clients to weigh and measure food. But, if you're eating as your diary says, I can only assume you're overeating the meats and dairy. So let's start weighing those, to eat no more than four ounces of meat or low-fat dairy at any meal. Do that for another week. You're not ready to expand to other foods yet."

Joan looks defeated. Luella has noticed that the only food-related symptom she's recorded is fatigue. But she obviously has body issues.

"Are you feeling depressed?" Luella asks.

"I guess so," Joan sighs. "This month is Mother's Day, which always hits me hard. I'm always thinking of questions I wish I could ask her. It sometimes feels like Mom's accident happens again every Mother's Day."

"Are you talking to your sister about this?"

"Yes. Cecilia and I don't live together anymore, but we share these thoughts."

"I'm glad you have each other. I'd like to see you get out and get moving. Walk. Swim. Consider seeing your doctor about depression but be aware that a side effect of many antidepression meds is often weight gain. So try exercise first this week to see if that helps."

"Thanks. I'll consider all this," Joan says as she gathers her things.

"Hang in there, my dear," Luella says.

Joan gives a sad grin, with a mock salute as she opens the door, and leaves. As she gets ready to leave, Luella mulls the session. *I'd like to keep some hope alive for Joan, but what is the mindset of someone who commits to wellness for her own good, then lies about what she's eating—while paying me to advise her? Sorta like Mom and her friends back in the day, smoking Virginia Slims as a diet aide and taking laxatives before their weekly weigh-in at Weight Watchers. It's like cheating at solitaire.*

4

Honestly, I'm Going to Lie to You/October 2012

Dante's learned not to meet first dates in a bar. Drinking only works to nullify good judgment and encourage sex with someone who's not yet vetted as a long-term prospect. This morning, he waits at Starbucks for Karla, who is a concierge at the Westin Hotel, claiming to be forty-three years old.

But you never know—there's probably a ten-year lying span. She's twenty minutes late, though she lives walking distance away, and he had to find parking. He's holding a table, waiting to order with her. Wishing he had something to read.

A brunette woman enters now—carrying her own drink into Starbucks—looking somewhat like her photo. Their eyes meet, and he waves at her. Walking over to his table, she says, "Dante, hi, I'm Karla." She seems surprised that he stood to shake her hand, which leads to her awkwardly setting down her cup to shake his. "I couldn't wait for coffee, so I brought my own. Go ahead and get what you want, and I'll save the table. If I need another cup, I'll get one later."

Dante tries not to be ticked off as the line's now much longer than when he came in. *I'll be waiting for my morning coffee a lot longer*, he thinks, getting up to go in line. When he finally sits down at the table, she says, "I needed coffee right away as I'm sleep deprived. My girlfriend and I went to hear Escape last night. Do you like music?"

"Yeah, but I'm not familiar with them."

"Oh, they're huge. Death metal. Lead guitarist lives in Sarasota. He's left-handed, plays a right-handed guitar upside down," she says. "Do you like death metal?"

"Sounds like quite a feat. I love music but can't do extremely loud. Too many decibels from long ago concerts damaged my hearing. I avoid live concerts now—not familiar with death metal music."

"Well, anyway," Karla continues, "by the time I got home, it was late." She takes a long sip of coffee. "But, honestly—I'd just as soon spend an evening watching TV, rather than going out every night."

A slight slurring of her 'jusssst as soon makes Dante wonder: *Is there something in her coffee? Is she still hanging onto last night's party time?*

"And once a week, I go to my investment club in my high-rise," Karla says.

"I've never been to one of those. Is it helpful?" Dante's grasping for something to talk about.

"It's great fun. I enjoy playing the market. Just made a huge bet on Macy's. They've been 'closing' stores— 'struggling'. But our leader thinks the 'odds' are their 'new efforts' and will hit it 'big'." She clicks her metallic fingernails on the table rhythmically, for emphasis. "They're planning to go into Dubai. And I have a hunch that REITS will pay off this year." Now rubbing her fingertips of one hand together to indicate money.

Dante's annoyed at her oddly colored nails, not quite gold. He can think of no reply to someone who uses gambling terms when discussing investing.

"But—honestly—I don't spend a lot of time thinking about money," Karla drains her coffee cup, and there's a silence. "I noticed you were an English major. How does that apply to working at a hardware store?"

Is she getting a little snarky? Dante wonders. "Well, it doesn't directly apply to hardware, of course. But literature applies to everything, as any English major will tell you." He laughs. "Are you a reader?"

"Yes! *Cosmo, Self.* Mainly magazines, as I have to do so much reading for work—tourist materials, local magazines."

Silence.

"Who are your favorite authors?" she asks.

"I like anything Grisham writes. Everything Richard Russo writes. Walter Mosely's detective stuff and Harlan Coben's legal thrillers." Silence. *Maybe cite some female authors*, Dante thinks. "And Kate Atkinson… Ann Tyler…" Karla's continued totally blank look leads him to say, "I've been spending a lot of time reading the Beatitudes lately."

"Is that fiction or nonfiction?" Karla asks.

"It's in a section of the Bible, along with what's called The Sermon on the Mount."

"I often say I'm an unappreciated minority. I was raised totally not religious. That often makes me unable to fit into what the rest of the world thinks or knows—or thinks it knows! Honestly—I think I had a deprived childhood." Karla says, grinning happily.

"Not so much a minority," Dante says, smiling. Stuffs his paper napkin into his empty cup.

"I'm gonna have to get to work, and probably you do too."

Neither gets a second cup of whatever they were drinking.

In the car, fastening his seat belt, Dante, thanks to Karla's gambling terms, recalls "The Rule of Chance." Applied to online dating, it would indicate that even a long streak of bad dates doesn't make him due for a good date. "Chance has no memory." Nor is it fair. Still, there must be some good potential dates out there.

He starts the car, lights a cigarette, and taps the AC button and the Elton John CD. At home, Mom plays Boticelli, Bartoli—all the Italian classical greats. She disdains the British singers her sons loved when growing up. In the car, Dante has it his way. "Let us live in peace," he sings with Elton while pulling out of the parking lot onto Tamiami Trail.

So I'll at least enjoy telling the girls about this date tonight, before The Apprentice. One-time English major Dante Moretti does love a good story, and—*for whatever reasons—the girls, at least, seem to feed on my sorry dating episodes.*

5

Harold's Shit Sandwich/November

Dante's left his car at the filling station on Main for an oil change, so he could return Mom's books to the library. Now walking back to his car, he's approaching a homeless man talking loudly on his cell. The man's age suggests he's one of the veterans on the street, probably 'Nam, likely suffers from PTSD. The guy's heading for the Orange St. roundabout and Dante—not wanting to startle him by coming up from behind and tapping him on the shoulder—jogs up to shadow him closely. Dante holds up his free hand to warn an approaching driver that this guy's dangerously distracted.

Dante—eyes heavenward—conveys to Lilliana, *We saved him, didn't we?* as he follows the guy up onto the curb.

Moving alongside the man who is now pocketing his phone, Dante says. "Hey, you just did something dangerous—talking on your cell while walking into roundabout traffic. I stopped a car from hitting you and kept others at bay till we got to the sidewalk." Dante mainly sees brownish gray hair while addressing this face: a scraggly head full to his shoulders, a bushy beard dipping partly over his upper lip.

"Oh, thanks, pal. I was on with the VA, trying to get an appointment. Need my meds."

"My wife was killed doing that," Dante says. "It's against the law now to drive while talking on a cell. But it's equally dangerous for pedestrians to do that."

"Jeez, I'm sorry, man. Thanks again. I'd like to say I owe ya, but"—shoulders shrugged, palms out—"I got nothin' to give?" They both laugh.

"Are you hungry?" Dante asks. "Can you join me for breakfast?"

"Sure." The guy extends his dirty hand, saying "I'm Harold."

Dante shakes Harold's filthy hand. "Dante. Pleased to meet you. Here's a good diner."

Dante had already eaten breakfast, but he knows that Harold wouldn't be seated if he came in alone. Dante plans to order a biscuit and coffee while encouraging Harold to get the Full Monty. After they order, Dante excuses himself to go to the bathroom, where he washes his hands. When he returns, Dante notices the man's dirty T-shirt indicates his military service.

"Thanks for your service, Harold. You were in 'Nam?"

"Yeah, long time ago, but I'm still in it."

"Jittery?"

Harold nods vigorously. "Loud noises—sirens, leaf blowers, helicopters—trigger it. Even after all these years. Wish I could settle down—up here." He taps his forehead. "Wish I could sleep. I was a squad commander. Value of life there was zilch. Strapping bombs to kids. When I lost guys, I felt it was my fault. Why them and not me? What do I say to their mom and dad? The numbers were horrific."

"Where was home back then?" Dante asks.

"Missouri. Home was just as bad. Just the other slice of bread on my shit sandwich. In St. Louis, I got off the plane in uniform, and a nice-looking lady spit on me. My best buddy came home and shot himself with his own weapon. I wondered if I could do it."

"I'm sorry," Dante says. They sit quietly, eating for a while. Then Dante asks, "What life had you wanted when you went into the service?"

"Wow. Who can remember? I guess the usual. Earn a good living. I married at nineteen, right before I went in. She left a different husband who returned from that hell. Don't blame her. I can't even imagine the life I dreamt of at that age. I live day to day. Just get by. There is no"—finger quotes—"home."

"Back in Missouri. Before 'Nam. What's your happiest memory?"

Harold seems to appreciate the challenge of this question. He stares at Dante, liking the guy who wants to know this. He forks his pancake and chews, staring into his distant past. He spears another bite of pancakes, then pauses to think, holding the food near his mouth, maple syrup dripping onto his beard.

After finishing that bite, Harold sips his coffee and says, "Springtime in Hermann, Missouri. When I was in high school. My stepdad used to lease an apple orchard, with a strawberry patch. Five thousand trees. We rented two hundred forty bee hives for a month, every spring, to pollinate. They came from Iowa on a flatbed trailer, in the middle of the night—twenty hives per pallet. My job was to be there when they unloaded."

"Just before dawn, I'd climb up into an apple tree and sit real still until the critters forgot I was there. After a few minutes—you wouldn't believe the noise of those bees—almost overwhelming. Busy, busy buzzin' in the apple blossoms. I could see pollen in the air. This was my favorite time all year."

"That scene you described—" Dante says. "—I'd love to see a National Geographic film of that."

"Me too!" Harold shows enthusiasm for the first time. "I'd visit the Iowans every year at Christmastime. We'd have apple blossom honey, then chew the beeswax like gum."

Both are heartened by this memory. Dante pays and gives Harold $10 so he can spend the night at Salvation Army, have a bed, and take a shower, with $3 left over. They shake hands, smile, and part. Walking back up Main Street, Dante recalls the Beatitude: "Blessed are the poor"—Jesus startling his listeners with the notion that the poor, the unclean, even crazy people have a place in God's kingdom.

Dante knows that the real sustenance of breakfast for Harold was conversation, being able to revisit who he'd once been. Street people all seem to have "meds" problems. Either not taking the ones they need or on drugs they shouldn't take, including—and especially—alcohol. Veterans may get eight-hundred-some dollars monthly, but that's not enough to rent a Sarasota apartment.

It does help that many self-medicate, probably Harold.

Dante realizes that buying Harold breakfast and a night of sleep doesn't qualify as his penance-good-deed—he's done that for street people before, but that beautiful image of a young Harold in his apple tree—*it's OK this doesn't count as penance.*

<h1 style="text-align:center">6</h1>

Barnum & Bailey and
Bonnie & Clyde/2012

Cecilia arrived at the Ritz Carlton two hours early, to find Donald Trump already there, posing for photos. Sarasota Republicans are giving Donald Trump their Statesman of the Year Award to raise money for Mitt Romney's presidential campaign. Cecilia hopes this fundraiser is so successful that they'll agree to pay her for future work.

On this sultry August evening, her admission to the photo ops—though not the dinner—is "payment" for her volunteer work. All indications are terrific. Attendees are paying $500 to get a photo taken with Trump! On top of their pricey seats for dinner.

"Hey there, Cecilia!" It's Barry, the campaign manager of Charlie Crist when he was governor, way back when Charlie was Republican. *Never seen Barry before in a necktie*, Cecilia thinks, *and he's grown some cute dark stubble. Against his fabulous skin tones. He's some kind of mixed-race.* Most people seem to be some type of biracial now.

Barry waves his hand to indicate that he wants her to move for a shot. "Squeeze into the background of one of those photo ops, and I'll take your picture next to Trump on the other guy's dime. For your grandchildren. You look more glamorous than these $1,000-a-plate wives."

Cecilia's confidence in her "seriously Republican yet sexy" black silk Anthropologie dress soars. *My killer silver necklace cost more than the dress, but it was worth the money. I'm happy to stand out from these Republican wives all wearing red.*

"OK." she laughs. "What are you doing here? Isn't Charlie an Independent now?"

"Yeah. But you know Charlie. When he comes to a fork in the road"—Barry makes a three-fingered fork—"he's apt to take every prong." Barry laughs. "Stay tuned."

"Surely Charlie's not moving to the Democrats!"

Barry makes a zipper-closing motion across his lips—over his smile, hinting yes.

"What *are* you doing here?" Cecilia asks.

"I'm here to shoot photos for my future grandchildren."

"You sure like to think ahead. You shoot me, and I'll shoot you. You believe our grandkids will know who Trump was?"

"Are you kidding? A showbiz billionaire who's Barnum & Bailey and Bonnie & Clyde? He'll be known long after all these other Republicans are forgotten."

The evening was a success in hoped-for and unexpected ways. The paper described Trump's speech as "fits of outrage and glee," which delighted attendees. He told the crowd that he was worth $8 billion—saying "Not bad, eh?"—and grinning at their hoots and applause.

"The next president needs to be a businessman, a winner. McCain was too nice to be president. Successful businessmen have beaten the hell out of people—they've won. And that makes enemies." *Is Trump talking about Romney here? Or himself?* Cecilia wonders.

A reporter wrote that it was probably the largest fund-raising dinner in Sarasota's history. Trump's sidekick Michael Cohen assured the reporter that "Trump has many deep thoughts on public policy."

Trump raised over $200,000 for Romney. Cecilia hopes to get a small share of that in future assignments. Billable time.

The next day, Barry and Cecilia text each other their photos. She sends one of Barry doing a Gangnam Style dance move, waving an invisible lasso.

TO: BarryCMgr@gmail.com
FROM: CeciliaPR@gmail.com
SUBJECT: Gangnam moves

Here's one for you to explain to your grandkids.

He responds with her Gangnam shot, calling to mind the Korean dancer's shout during those dance craze videos.

TO: CeciliaPR@gmail.com
FROM: BarryCMgr@gmail.com
SUBJECT: Sexy Laaaa-dy!

That night, he texts her the front page of a 1992 tabloid about Trump dumping his first wife, an immigrant from the

Czech Republic. The paper's headline was "Trump Bounces Czech."

TO: CeciliaPR@gmail.com
FROM: BarryCMgr@gmail.com
SUBJECT: Trump Dump

How about dinner to catch up on our political endeavors? Friday? Or whenever?

TO: BarryCMgr@gmail.com
FROM: CeciliaPR@gmail.com
SUBJECT: Friday's fine
Looking forward. C.

I'd like to get Barry's advice about moving into paid work, she thinks. And find something new to wear to dinner with him. Memories of her last boyfriend Nathan—who the family still refer to as "Nothin" or "the bartender"—make Barry look very good.

7

Intermittent Explosive Disorder/January 2013

The NPR report of Barack Obama being sworn in for a second term makes Sidney Abramson think of his college days. Most University of Chicago grad students in social work in the '70s were reading Alinsky's *Rules for Radicals*. Community organizing was taught, but it seemed more like volunteer work than a career. Then in the '80s, a guy gets a paying job as a community organizer—in Chicago!—and goes on to become president. *Who knew? Could I have been a contender?* He pulls into his parking spot and continues to listen.

Dr. Ben Carson—newly retired from medicine and now a GOP presidential contender—has linked Alinsky and Obama to Satan—"the first radical...rebelling against the establishment...who won his own kingdom." Sid smiles at the excitement of that road not taken. His longtime career as a therapist has been quiet, serving Sarasotans able to spend $120 an hour for help dealing with loss, anxiety, depression, sometimes boredom.

A woman in a gray Hyundai pulling in beside his black BMW must be the new client appointment: Something Cohen. "Ms. Cohen?" he asks, as she steps out.

She replies, "Yes. I'm Luella. You must be Sidney Abramson?"

He escorts her into his office, offers her one of two club chairs, and sits in the other. A Kleenex is popped up in the box on the coffee table between them.

"What brings you here today?" The opener.

"I guess you could say it's what I'm doing with my life. I've been a nutritionist for twelve years now, and I've become impatient with most of my clients, and I dislike some. Of course, I hide my feelings all day. I have to ask you: have you ever really disliked certain clients?"

Sidney laughs. "I'll admit some are more challenging than others. But no," he lies. "I've never actually disliked a client. How long has this been going on? And do you find certain types of clients especially difficult?"

"Ah…three, maybe four years. And, yes, it's the liars that bug me. Which seems to be most of them."

"Really? Can you give me an example?"

"I've been seeing a woman for years. From a wealthy Sarasota family."

Bragging, Sidney thinks. *Hoping I'll try to guess who these wealthy Sarasotans are.*

"Her aunt is a drama queen—a tantrum-throwing woman—gets tossed out of restaurants."

Intermittent explosive disorder, Sidney thinks, *5.5% to 7.5% of the population.*

"This volatile woman lost a lot of weight, then decided to renew her wedding vows—mainly so she could wear a bridal gown."

Sidney finds this oddly familiar.

"Catholics have these marriage vow renewal ceremonies," Luella continues. "But not because you lose weight! Though I don't get that whole idea of renewing vows anyway. Does 'til death do us part' expire—before death?"

"Perhaps it's the Catholic priests who should be renewing their vows?" Sidney smiles.

Luella laughs a "Yes!" and continues. "Her husband had a brief affair with their caterer, then cut it off quickly. The wife works out to get slim for the vow renewal, then gains all her weight—and more—back. My client who told me this story says when her uncle was at the caterer's and asked if she were free, the caterer said—flirting while actually warning him—'The truth will set you free. But, first, it will break your heart.' He got involved with her anyway."

Nick Moretti! Sidney realizes. *My former client. But she's wrong: what the caterer said to Nick was "I'm not free, but I'm very reasonable." Best pickup line I've ever heard. And Nick learned later that his high-maintenance wife's activities with her personal trainer were not just at the gym. Nor was the working out.*

Sidney shares office space and an appointment book with his colleague Sheila, so he knows that Sheila's now counseling Rosemary Moretti *That wife who throws the shit fits is Sheila's case, thank god.*

Wondering about Luella's distorted broken-hearted twist on the incident, Sid asks, "Do any of your personal relationships help fortify you against what seems to be professional burn-out?"

"Not now. My wife is divorcing me. Fourteen years together; then last year when Florida made gay marriage legal, we tied the knot. So we got the freedom to marry—and the consequences. Now I'm in half of marriages that divorce. What made us think we'd beat the odds?"

"The law set you free—and then broke your heart?" Sidney offers.

Not acknowledging his echo of her story, Luella talks of how clients lie about fulfilling tasks and about what they eat and drink.

Nick was uncomfortable cheating, so he broke off the affair quickly, which was difficult, Sidney recalls. *Later, he learned that his wife was cheating. He even wondered if back when they renewed their marriage vows she was hoping that it might renew their marriage relationship.*

Nick brought his anger and grief to me. They finally divorced.

Luella's voice is getting whiney as she talks on and on.

Sidney reviews treatment plans: Explore Luella taking time off: vacation. What (if anything) gives her pleasure now? Or once did? Task to explore other careers and bring findings here weekly. She's sounding depressed: Rx? Would like to tackle that whining too.

Glancing at his watch, Sid says: "Going to have to end in a few minutes."

The shifting Moretti story reminds Sidney of the analyst's mantra: "If you change the way you look at things, the things you look at change." *Wonder how Nick's doing these days. Nice guy.*

8

Free Enterprise/April

In the warm steam of her morning shower, Cecilia thinks fondly of her former high school class on the Constitution. Her teacher, Mrs. Young, gave Cecilia her first experience of fitting in with others, with purpose. Taking stands on issues of the day—from abortion to gay marriage. At her Catholic school, religious faith could have no part in arguments in Mrs. Y's room. They had to be Constitution-based. *As if we were Supreme Court judges.*

Cecilia took a right-to-die position in the Terri Schiavo case. Terri's husband wanted to take his wife off her fifteen-year feeding tube support; her parents—hoping Terri would emerge from her coma—fought him, ending in a trial to determine Terri's own wishes (which had never been made clear in any document). After the judge ruled in favor of the husband in 2005, Florida Governor Jeb Bush moved it to a Federal Court; President George W. Bush advocated moving it to the Supreme Court; and it became the final test in Mrs. Y's room. The ultimate verdict mirrored Cecilia's argument: remove the feeding tube.

Then an autopsy showed that Terri's brain had deteriorated to half a normal size. No treatment could have

41

ever pulled her out of that state. As shampoo suds circle the drain, Cecilia recalls learning that some things can be worse than death.

Shutting off the water and grabbing her towel, she rubs her hair with vigor, thinking of that year that was all about the need for—and the price of—freedom, and showing her a talent she didn't know she had. That how exciting such work could be *while living in a home where we're not allowed to discuss politics!*

Cecilia's work that high school summer was with a Florida preservation group. When a board member ran for county commissioner, she put his campaign sign in the front yard. *And Dad took it down—saying some Ace customers vote the other way. Ousted again!*

Hair dryer noise shuts out all but her thoughts about what Mrs. Y might think about Libertarians, assuming she'd like their support for a free market and for personal freedom. *She'd understand my wanting to explore getting work from them while trying to do good in the world.*

Roger Spaw, regional director of Florida's Libertarian Party, eagerly awaits his appointment with Cecilia Moretti. Google indicates that she's of the Ace Hardware family, so, well-to-do. She seems interested in joining but wants to talk first. *Hope she doesn't know we lost one of her shirttail relatives recently, over a situation that could have been avoided. If only I'd known.*

Stacks of paper spill from shelves in his small home office and spread in small piles over his desk. It's a hard-working, committed volunteer's domain. Through the window, he sees Cecilia pulling the metallic silver Subaru she shares with Nani into the driveway. He heads to the door and opens it before she has to ring.

"Welcome. I'm Roger. Come on in."

"Hello. Thank you for seeing me on short notice."

He motions her to the chair across from his desk and, settling into his own chair, smiles and says, "Of course, I'm eager to know what brings you to us."

"Well, I'm a registered Republican," Cecilia says, "who's long shared Libertarian values—reducing debt, reforming taxes and entitlements."

"We're certainly on board with those values," Roger says, smiling.

"I like the Libertarian's 'live-and-let-live' views of personal decisions about abortion, gender preference, and the like. So I just don't know about Trump. Sarasota's Republicans are planning to name him 'Statesman of the Year' again. 'Statesman' doesn't seem to capture whatever he is!"

"I appreciate how this has been brewing with you. Was there any specific turning point?"

"Yes. I ran into my Aunt Rosemary at the library last week. We hadn't seen each other in years—she's divorced from my uncle. I told her I had my own website design business, and she was also launching a business. Before we parted, she led me into the stacks and pulled out *How I Found Freedom in an Unfree World*. Saying 'You gotta read this.' I did, and that brought me here."

"Ah, a golden oldie. Author Harry Browne was once a Libertarian Presidential candidate." Roger's smile is just from the nose down, though.

He caught his breath when she mentioned the volatile Rosemary Moretti. At one time, Roger had recommended Ayn Rand to Rosemary. She started with that novel *The Fountainhead. Came here to throw a hissy-fit, screaming, "Her hero rapes a woman in the first few pages. And she falls in love with him? And marries him! How can any decent person recommend this assault on women?" Threw the book at me. I had no idea she'd start with a 1940s novel—not Rand's finest work, by any measure.*

Cecilia continues, "I'm taking Browne's advice and would like to discuss offering my website and design services—as a volunteer at this point—for whatever projects you'd like to discuss. Then, if you like what I do and if the party has any design needs, we might move to a financial agreement. Or not. Either way, I'd like to be involved in the Party. As an independent contractor, I find that everything Browne says about self-employment and self-reliance rings true to me."

"Great! Needless to say, I agree whole-heartedly," Roger says. "Polls now show that we're on the cusp of a major movement. I expect we'll need banners and other materials for our national convention. Let me find out where the committee is on those matters, and we'll set up a meeting to get your ideas and input."

"I'd also like to draft a design for your website. Your reaction—positive or negative—will help me know your sensibilities and experience." She rises from the chair. "Thank you. I'm so pleased to have had this discussion."

Walking her to the door, Roger says, "We'll welcome your participation." *A Moretti check would be welcome too.* There won't be any more $10,000 checks from Auntie Rosemary to Florida's Libertarian Party.

###

Cecilia has often wished to discuss politics at home, but the demonizing that fills such discussions online and among people today is off-putting. *At least, Dad's kept us from that.*

Libertarians don't try to push their views onto others either. Maybe Dad shares their "live-and-let-live" policy.

Still, she found Roger underwhelming. She'd like to put some sizzle in their media presence and promotional materials. After long being the family's undeclared GOP elephant in the room, Cecilia's now morphing into whatever the Libertarian animal would be. One that would stand out as an individual. Maybe the Great White Shark? Among the few creatures that prefer to be alone—not swimming together to hunt prey, nor forming a group for survival as most animals do.

She has no exclusivity agreements with her Republican clients. *No reason I can't work for both. When you come to a fork in the road, take it! Harry Browne would call that freedom.* She goes to the Florida Libertarian Party's website and makes a $250 donation to remind Roger Spaw to discuss her with the committee. Their site needs—desperately!—to be updated.

Getting up to brew a cup of tea, Cecilia thinks of Barry still working for Charlie Crist, who's now a Democrat.

Wonder how Barry would react to me as a Libertarian. If I would share that. Secret political affiliation is my family's policy. Barry doesn't seem hard-and-fast any party. Him knowing this shouldn't be a deal-breaker. Should it?

After Barry had once compared their relationship to that of Mary Matalin and James Carville, Cecilia googled to find that Carville was Bill Clinton's Democrat campaign manager when Matalin was steering his Republican opponents, both Bush presidents. They've been married since 1993, have two kids, and "don't talk politics at home." *Just like us! I've never known another family like ours.*

Cecilia often wonders if being the outlier in the family is an inborn trait. *If so, when trying to stand out, why do I so long to fit in? Aren't those longings mutually exclusive? No one wants to be lonely. Do they? Not counting the Great White Shark.*

An email pops up—from Aunt Rosie:

TO: CeciliaPR@gmail.com
FROM: RosemaryCLC@yahoo.com

Great to see you @ library. Hope you enjoy "Finding Freedom…" Good luck with freelancing. Below is my new adventure.

Cecilia clicks on Rosemary's link: "Cognitive, Physical & Emotional Wellness" site. Rosemary Moretti has become a Certified Life Coach! Cecilia texts this startling news. Her subject line has only an emoji:

TO: JoanAceHW@srq.com
cc DanteAceHW@srq.com
FROM: CeciliaPR@gmail.com
SUBJECT:

9

Barbershop Confessions/2014

Dante sits in Alberti's Barbershop on Main Street, waiting for a haircut with Jimmy, who came here from Sicily decades ago. He sees that *TIME*'s upcoming "Persons of the Year" cover will be "The Ebola Fighters." A man who'd tested positive for Ebola in Liberia lied to get on a plane to Dallas, then stayed with a woman and her kids in a densely populated Dallas neighborhood. Misdiagnosed in ER; sent home with useless medicine; sent back to ER; another doctor diagnoses America's first Ebola case, then quickly isolates one-hundred-seventy-seven of the patient's contacts. When it was over, eleven Americans survived Ebola; two were his nurses.

Only the Liberian died.

Like a horror movie, Dante thinks. *We missed a virus that ravaged Africa and Europe by the skin of our teeth because one guy in the ER knew what to activate immediately.*

Jimmy calls, "Hey, Dante, over here," indicating the waiting barber chair.

Dante sits, saying "I've been wondering if I should just shave it all off"—sweeping a hand over his bald head—"get rid of it all."

"Well, you got three choices," Jimmy says. "Chrome Dome, like you just said, Michael Jordan look. Or you can keep the Fringe Semi-Circle you have now, trimmed up neatly. Or I'll give you the Donald Do—like Trump, which costs ten times as much as either of those. More if we dye it orange."

"Eliminating the Donald, what do you think?" Dante asks.

"Well, you've got the shape head and broad face for a total shave. That style is not so good for skinny guys with egg-shaped heads. But…you've got a strong jaw and your salt-and-pepper semicircle has a nice texture and kinda softens your face. It's really a personal decision." Another customer and his barber, listening, seem to agree.

"What's sexiest?" Dante includes the other two in his laugh. "I'm thinking of maybe changing my dating site photo."

The other chair's customer looks over to advise Dante, "You need to go to another dating website, post the new photo there, and see which the ladies prefer." That guy's barber, George, likes this idea.

"Ah, let's just do the regular trim. Don't know if I'm up to branching out to experiment at this point. Or just throw in the towel," Dante says.

Jimmy begins the trim. "No luck dating?"

"I've been told men lie about their height—which I don't need to do—but women lie about everything! Starting with their photo—often taken ten or more years earlier. What you see is *not* what you get!"

The other customer, now reclining, lifts the hot towel covering his just-shaved face. "When you make the date give her a condition—'If you don't look like your photo, you're buying the drinks until you do.'" The men hoot and holler in agreement.

"You're not the first who's telling me this stuff," Jimmy says. "Other lies you've been told…?"

"A Jehovah's Witness, recruiting. And that's just one of the lesser deceptions."

"Worse than an evening of *that*?" Jimmy says while clipping.

"One gal who wants to take me to a fancy dinner, tux required. I figure it's a fund-raiser, and—what the hell— find out what kinda causes she supports. Which tells a lot. Right?"

"And, the charity is…?"

"Not a charity at all. It was a wedding. Recently—and bitterly—divorced, this gal wanted me only for that one [finger quotes] 'date'."

"Did she ask you to go in on the gift?" More laughter all around.

"I was a sucker for that worthy cause lie because of a confession—long time ago. Hadn't been in maybe twenty years, so it wasn't a short confession! I'm expecting a penance, proportionate. Third-world priest. And he tells me to do a good deed."

"Unusual. So what deed did you do?" Jimmy asks, shaving Dante's neck.

"That's the problem. What qualifies? Every good deed I do tends to be something I'd have done anyway. I can't figure out what would count as my penance. So I thought maybe that girl's supposed fundraiser might lead me to a good cause I didn't know about."

"Maybe everlasting penance was the priest's intention. I heard of such a thing once. A bartender who always muttered when he was pouring drinks. After years of watching this, a regular customer asks him why he mumbles to himself when he's pouring wine." Jimmy brushes Dante's neck. "The bartender says that as a fourteen-year-old altar boy, he confessed to drinking some communion wine when he was back of the altar putting on his cassock. Priest so angry; he gave him a penance that from now on he's to say a 'Hail Mary' every time he pours a glass of wine. Forever."

"And he became a bartender?" Dante asks.

"Yep. Go figure." Jimmy pulls the cape away. Done.

Dante pays and leaves. Walking up Main Street, he thinks about how Catholics talk about their confessions. Seven sacraments and the one people tell the most stories about is Confession. The only one whose very nature is supposed to involve secrecy.

###

After his haircut, Dante walks down the street to the independent bookstore. Mom wants *Killing Kennedy* and *Unbroken*, and he recently ordered Michael Connelly's legal thriller *The Brass Verdict* as well as a nonfiction—*The Divine Conspiracy*. That author died recently, and after reading he'd been a philosophy professor at UCLA, Dante thinks this book may offer a fresh look at *The Sermon on the Mount*. The other part of his long-ago penance.

Later, walking with the bag of books, Dante anticipates the pleasure of reading a new book this evening—*will it be mystery writer Connelly? Or the Baptist teacher on the mystery of Matthew's Gospel?* Whenever Dante has two new books, he reads the first page of each to decide which to start on this most enjoyable dilemma.

He approaches the police station, and Dante's thoughts turn to his cringeworthy appointment with Chief Bernadette DiPino. He gets clearance to go up to her office, where she stands in the doorway, waiting. She leads him to her desk, upon which stands the Angel Michael, patron of police officers, Dante recalls.

"So nice to see you, Dante," she says. "How's Angelina? Haven't seen your mom in some time."

"Great. Busy making biscotti for church weddings, as always."

Sitting in the chair indicated, Dante sees a photo that he realizes is a DiPino family picture with the chief at her daughter's swearing-in ceremony. Two older policemen are standing by them. "Is that your dad and grandfather also there?" he asks, pointing to the men in uniform.

"Yep. All four generations in uniform. Our fifth generation was deceased by then," the chief says. "You appreciate a family business, of course."

"Yes. But we're just three generations in hardware, so a long way to go to get to the DiPino level." All business now, Dante says, "I'm here to tell you the most bizarre story you'll hear all day."

"I'm all ears," the chief says, eyebrows raised, smiling.

"I've been playing a computer word game for several months," Dante says. "You're playing with people from everywhere—anywhere!—and there's a back room where you can chat privately with another player. I started chatting backstage with a woman—mainly snarking about two other players who irritated us both."

"We became gamer friends. Then she suggested we exchange pictures. This surprised me, because…why? Her picture's gorgeous. After that, she offered to come here from Miami to meet. When I met her, she was as gorgeous as the photo. One thing led to another, and…" He waves his hand in circles, indicating "and so on."

"Yeah, I'm getting it," the chief says. "Can't wait for the punch line."

"After our intimate encounter, she suddenly bursts into tears. Confesses she's married although she'd claimed to be single in our online chats. Says her 'very wealthy' husband is brutal. She fears for her life. Wishes he was dead, as she has nothing to live on if they divorce. He's supposedly so well connected he'd get everything. Otherwise, she'd get it all, and there's hefty life insurance too. She just wishes him dead."

"Trying to recruit you," the chief says.

"Pretty obvious about it. I indicated I had no interest. When she departed, we both knew we wouldn't be communicating again," Dante said. "So I felt maybe I should…dump this in your lap!" They both laugh. "Just what do you do with something like this?"

"The first thing I do is tell you to stay out of backroom chat spaces," the chief says. "As you've found out, all kinds of bad folks lurk there. Even if they're smart word game players. Or beautiful."

"I hear you," Dante says. "And will abide by your order for the rest of my days."

"However, since this is a serious matter, I'm going to ask for your cooperation to stay in touch with her," the chief says. "If she's planning what it looks like, we need to prevent that."

"Holy cannoli!" Dante says. "I told her I had no interest in pursuing this, which meant we had no reason to stay in touch. That was a couple weeks ago. It was an unfriendly parting."

"I suggest you see if you can act like you're rethinking it, see if you can reopen the issue," she says. "She may think you're rethinking the money. We'll work with you on any response you may get—guide you toward getting information. Eventually, we'll take it from there."

The surprised Dante is shaken. *I expected her to hand this over to the Miami cops where that girl's from.* "OK. I'll see what I can do." He exhales a big, somewhat frightened "Whew!"

"Maybe you should just try Match.com," the chief says, smiling.

"Been there, done that. I'll spare you those stories!" Getting up to leave, Dante walks to the door, then remembers—"I had a long chat today with Harold, a 'Nam Veteran on the streets. You know him?"

"Yeah. He's not been a problem. Keeps mostly to himself. Drinks."

"Is there any help for PTSD around here?"

"Florida Veterans organization has a program." She hands him her card and says, "Check them out online, and if you have any further questions about him, let me know. He has to want to do it, and it will involve AA. Sounds like a gigantic step for him."

"Forewarned! Just want information. Thanks."

"Speaking of other matters," the chief says, "there was an incident recently with Rosie Moretti."

He groans. "What's she done now?"

"She's infuriated about the proposed condo construction next door to her downtown high-rise. At City Commission meetings, she gets so riled up and insulting— we had to escort her out last Monday. I agree that particular approval may be problematic. But—you know—the meetings are to hear the pros and cons, and developers come prepared to have their case heard. It's not that Rosemary doesn't have a good argument; it's that she can't *give* a good argument."

"How well my family knows. I'm sorry she's become your problem—but sure glad she's no longer ours!"

"She's the least of my problems!" the chief says. "Just keeping you up to date."

Dante is thoroughly rattled on his drive home. He hadn't anticipated being asked to reignite communication with this plotting woman—Natalie. This is an unexpected good deed from out of the blue—*one I desperately don't want to do! Getting back in touch with the beautiful, nasty Natalie is too much! But there's no choice. Gotta think of the poor jerk who married her. The chief is counting on me. Shit!*

He walks back to his car and unloads the books on the front passenger seat. Flips open the glove compartment and gets out his pack of Natural American Spirit cigarettes. He knows that "organic, addictive-free" tobacco is oxymoronic. That tobacco is poison. He's been tapering down. But a bad day recalling his sorry dating history—ending in a horrifying good deed assignment—calls for a cigarette, if anything does.

Lighting up, he takes a satisfyingly guilty inhale, blows smoke out an open window, and drives toward home. He recalls his first date, two years after being widowed. *Robin. Only woman my age in the grief support group. Both of us still mourning too much to move on. But there's been no one that close to what I think we might have had, in all these years since. Is this just wishful thinking about something that wasn't even tried?*

He's come to the point of needing to cut the time and cost of dating. A first date has to be great—not just so-so, to warrant a second. Avoid meaningless chatter, which is usually flirting, leading to sex, which blinds you to the deal-breaker differences. *At the barbershop, Jimmy calls that foreploy: misleading for the purpose of getting laid.*

Dante turns into his driveway wondering: Why is dating not any fun? *Why am I facing the worst Good Deed imaginable?—definitely, the first one I'd never come up with on my own.*

He enters through the garage.

Once in the house, he goes directly to his bedroom, gets out of his shoes, then peels off his clothes. He pulls on his

Tampa Bay Buccaneers' pewter gray sweatpants and a T-shirt in the teams' odd red-orange-black-pewter color scheme—which does look piratical. Sitting at the corner desk in his bedroom, he opens his computer, knowing he needs to do it now rather than dread it for days and allow it to distract him from reading a good book tonight. His addiction to books at least is not only legal but shared by everyone he cares about.

She's not in the game. So no backroom chit-chat. He has her email, so texts the nasty Natalie: "Can we talk?"

That's enough for today. Relieved, Dante opens his two books to read the first pages and decide which book he'll start tonight after dinner.

First, he reads Connelly's brief opening page of *The Brass Verdict.*

He reads it quickly, then sits back to think.

Connelly seems to be saying that everyone at a trial is a liar. Lawyers, cops, victims, witnesses. He's patient, knowing this, waiting for the lie that will break open the trail. To be the truth amid liars.

Wow. Knowing Connelly's skill at tackling such stuff in surprising ways, Dante opens *The Divine Conspiracy*. Its Introduction promises to offer a fresh understanding of Jesus, whom most people—incorrectly, the author claims—fit only in the categories of dogma and law. Instead, Jesus and his words are essentially subversive of established arrangements and ways of thinking.

Two enticing books, Dante thinks. *Both authors saying the world has got it wrong, and my job is to set it right.* He sets the books down on his nightstand side by side. He'll decide after dinner which comes first—the mystery writer tackling a story about the nature of man. Or the Baptist teacher tackling the nature of the man Jesus—and how that might relate to his long-ago penance?

Finding it impossible to choose between them on an empty stomach, Dante looks forward to reading whichever appeals to his greatest need or his native curiosity at the end of this challenging day.

10

If I Could Ask Mom One Question April/2015

They brought Grandmother Angelina Moretti's ashes home; the funeral will be in June, in the old New Hampshire parish, with burial next to Grandfather Dominic. Tonight, Joan's coming back to sleep with Cecilia in the room they shared as children. Nani's death was sad for Dad, but the girls share a mutual grief: they've lost their other mother. After Mom's accident, Nani had come from up north to help out "for a time," which turned out to be the rest of her life.

Their mother Lilliana had been born in Italy, an only child. The girls met grandparents Messina only three times, the last at Mom's funeral sixteen years ago. Then both grandparents died within two years. Nani became their advisor, teacher, and cheerleader. *But Nani was more than that to me*, Cecilia thinks. *She was the only one I didn't disappoint. She didn't fret about what I should become, she loved me as is, full throttle. We had such fun—everywhere, even in the kitchen. I don't have a whit of her cooking skills, and she didn't care. The only thing she expected of me was a good time, laughing at* Curb Your Enthusiasm. *Whatever. Just being together.*

Joan enters, wearing a sleep shirt, plunks a backpack on the dresser, and stretches out on her childhood bed. "Some day, huh?" The girls find comfort in their old twin beds, looking out the window at the diminishing light of the setting sun.

"We're never gonna hear, 'Tony, Tony, come around: something's lost and can't be found' again," Cecilia citing Nani's frequent plea. In her last years, Nani was always hunting for glasses, keys, the checkbook, asking St. Anthony, Patron of Lost Things, to help find them.

"Mom called on saints too," Joan said. "Remember St. Jude, Patron of Impossible Causes?"

"She'd be multi-tasking like mad, juggling orchestra rehearsals, teaching, all she did at home and our school. That last year, planning all of us going to Italy to hear her string quartet. See our grandparents there. Her quartet still fretting about selections, and she was working on flights to Milan that awful day. Constantly on her cell. Unfortunately."

"Yeah. Mom and Nani were probably the only people in Sarasota—even at St. Armand's Circle—who knew that St. Armand is the Patron Saint of Bartenders," Cecilia says. "My namesake's so obvious. Good old Cecilia, Patron of Music, unfortunate choice for me. But you came first and— was she thinking Joan of Arc? That French girl they burned at the stake?"

"I've always wanted to ask her that! The Inquisition excommunicates Joan and burns her alive. Then centuries later their successors say: 'Ooooops! Our bad! She was a saint. Let's canonize her!'"

"Those men had troubles with women—even a teenager—way back then," Cecilia says. "I read that one of the charges against her was cross-dressing. Did they expect her to wear a lady's gown—on horseback? Leading an army? Sidesaddle?"

"It's her suit of armor they found too uppity," Cecilia says, and they laugh. "Old celibate priests judging women! Remember Nani telling us that the pill was invented by a Catholic doctor—who was dismayed when the Vatican condemned it?" Cecilia says. "Nani's generation took it without asking permission. And without confessing it."

"She wanted us to know that history but didn't talk about it in the present time," Joan said. "We knew how to get it, but some advice about when to start it and who with would have been helpful."

"Yeah. She made us responsible, but not smart! Leroy Riley. Ugh. What was I *thinking*?"

"Conrad Snyder. I thought the first boy taller than me qualified him. Wrong!" Joan said. There's a lull.

Cecilia thinks of how much easier Joan's relationship with Mom was. *Joan doesn't have the talent or the patience for music. I had the talent and patience, but not the guts. Vomiting before recitals. Mom said I'd outgrow performance anxiety. I wanted not to have to be expected to. I disappointed her. Joan has an easier relationship with Dad too, following in his footsteps. Seems like I've spent all my life looking for the path I'm destined to take.*

Softly, she asks Joan, "Remember when we started: 'If I Could Ask Mom One Question' ?"

"Yeah, 'cause my first one was: 'Do you have bad cramps during your period like I do?'"

"Mine were mostly about navigating middle school. Nasty girl bullies. Later I wanted to ask 'How old were you when you knew you wanted to make the violin your career? Did you consider anything else?'" Cecilia recalls her struggle between majoring in business or political science. Or even art and design, which might have been most helpful of all of them.

"And all those other questions we wondered if girls did ask their moms: 'How did you lose your virginity? When? Did you ever do grass?'" Joan says.

"And how did you know Dad was the one you wanted to spend the rest of your life with?" Cecilia says.

"This year, I most want to know: 'What size shoe did you wear?'" Joan raises both legs up to stare at her feet. "I don't know any other woman who wears my size twelve. Mom was 5'11", and I'd like to think she wore a size twelve shoe too."

"So shallow," Cecilia said, laughing, while aware that this is about Joan's body anxiety.

"I'm not shallow," Joan says, "I'm thick. At 6'2", the big foot monster."

"You're *not*! Have you forgotten Nani's list of famous women six feet tall—to make you stand proud? Brooke Shields…Taylor Swift…"

They banter the names. "Allison Janney…Geena Davis…"

"Nicole Kidman…Sigourney Weaver…"

"Venus Williams…and speaking of athletes, Kaitlyn Jenner. A special case." They laugh.

"And a gorgeous 6'2"," Joan adds, "just like me, only way better looking."

Cecilia says, "This year my question to Mom would be 'Who will you vote for?' Do you think Mom and Dad voted alike? He won't talk politics." She imitates a stentorian Dante: "'Political opinions are like noses. We all have them—some are bigger than others. But it's never OK to wipe your nose on another person's sleeve.'"

"Aaargh," says Joan.

"Sounds like they differed, doesn't it?"

"I can't recall anything about politics at home back then. I suspect it's Dad and Nani who differed—and perhaps still do," Joan says.

"I'll bet you're right! Well, if Mom were here today, I'd want to know if she'd go for Obama or McCain. What she thinks about the Tea Party. Or the influence of billionaires, like Trump and Bloomberg. Exciting or scary?"

Suddenly, Joan sits straight up in the bed. "Oh my god! I forgot. I was supposed to call the church so we can let Nani's friend Frances know. Since the funeral will be later in New Hampshire, no one at the church here will know that Nani died."

Cecilia gasps: "Franny will be expecting her to come to bake biscotti this week. We gotta let her know."

"I'll call and leave a message asking someone to call me first thing tomorrow. Franny's been grandma's best friend since she moved to Sarasota. Nani passing away is gonna be as much of a shock to her as it was to us."

The next morning, Joan and Cecilia linger at the breakfast table after Dad leaves. Cecilia gets up to clear the table, and Joan's cell phone rings. "It's the church," she says, moving out to the patio. Cecilia's loading the dishwasher minutes later, when Joan returns, her jaw dropped.

"There are no special Italian weddings with food at St. Martha's Church. The pastor's from Italy, but there's not even a significant bunch of Italians there. Their biggest ethnic group is Vietnamese. Grandma and Francis never baked biscotti for church during those sleepovers. Francis Bisignano is a man."

They stand there and look at each other while this sinks in.

"Holy shit!" Cecilia says.

"Why would Nani do this?"

"No idea."

"So. We gotta tell Dad."

###

Dante's working the floor at an Ace in Longboat Key. His red vest says "Dante" but not "Owner." Helping on the floor occasionally keeps him informed of customer preferences and can shed light on the operation of an individual store. He follows a customer in a jacket that indicates he's with a Wounded War Veteran's organization. Dante wheels his purchase out to his car, wanting to ask about resources for Harold, who's now getting counseling for PTSD and is back to AA after falling off the wagon twice.

64

Dante wonders—assuming Harold gets clean—*what could be his future? Can we get him off the street?* This customer tells him the organization must limit its assistance to today's wounded warriors, but he listens with interest to Dante's story of Harold. He gives Dante his card, asking him to call when Harold's able to work.

That exchange is making Dante run late, which means Friday traffic back to town's going to be hell. But that WWV contact may be helpful someday.

He'd called Chief DiPino today to report that Natalie has ghosted him. She's dropped out of the game room for good and hasn't replied to any of his texts. The chief says they'll probably call in the FBI to take it from here. She thanks him for trying. Such relief! *I did my duty, and it's in the hands of the police now. That's surely the worst possible thing I'll have to deal with this year.*

###

The girls are antsy, waiting to tell the news. Though it isn't a TV night, they're sitting in the loveseat in the TV area because they planned to order pizza after Dad gets home.

Facing the TV are Dante's Italian leather chestnut colored recliner and Angelina's stain-and-fashion-repellent 'plush' fabric recliner, now faded from its once coal black. Between the recliners, the girls sit on a down-cushioned loveseat upholstered in "white with a whisper of green" their mom had once said of its breezy color.

Joan brought two bottles of extravagant Barolo and placed them on the massive coffee table. She and Cecilia have started sampling.

"Do you think we should have invited Uncle Nick, too?" Cecilia says. "He might have some idea of what Nani was thinking."

"It's hard enough for just us to get together at the end of a workday—and Dad's late now. Dad will tell him after we talk—get his ideas about this. So strange that Nani—who talked to us freely about birth control and sex—would have been prudish about whatever relationship they had during those sleepovers."

"Yeah. Such deliberate deception. For what possible reason?" They hear the garage door going up.

Entering the kitchen, Dante looks surprised to see Joan here in her Ace vest, which means she came directly from her store. It's not a TV night, but they're sitting in the TV area.

"Hey," he says dropping his keys in the dish. "Everything OK?" He walks to join them, noticing the empty wineglass in the glass holder on his lounge chair's arm. Joan gets up from the loveseat to pour.

"We thought we'd order pizza tonight after you got home," Cecilia says, walking toward the kitchen to place the order. That explains the seating. Nani claimed that her family of readers needed this huge coffee table for magazines, books, and the newspaper's crossword puzzles.

She'd never allow it to be used for a store-bought pizza.

After pouring Dante's wine, Joan says, "We found out something when I talked to the receptionist at St. Martha's Church." She sits to give him the news: "Nani's friend

'Franny' is a man named Francis Bisignano. There was no biscotti baking for the church those nights she slept over."

Dante's stunned. "What the hell…? Why…?"

"I know. That seems so unlike her. I think of Nani as so direct. Can't fathom any reason she'd have hidden whatever relationship she had with him."

"Unless it has to do with Mr. Bisignano," Dante says. "Something she didn't want us to know."

"Maybe he's married?" Joan says.

"I don't think Mom would ever have been a party to something like that all these years," says Dante. "Something else. For whatever reason, she didn't want to introduce him to us." It wasn't until his second glass of wine and the pizza's arrival that Dante said what they'd almost forgotten: "There's an old man in Sarasota expecting Mom to come to his house Monday night. Something important—to them— all this time. I've got to let him know she died."

###

May I Be Perfectly Frank with You?

Nani had told them Mr. Bisignano lives walking distance to Church, just off Orange Street, so his house is was easy to find that Saturday. They decided Cecilia should go along, perhaps looking less threatening than a strange unannounced man ringing his doorbell.

The door opens, and they see eyeglasses, above a chain. An elderly voice says, "Can I help you?"

"Mr. Bisignano, I'm Dante Moretti, Angelina's son, and this is my daughter Cecilia. May we come in?"

The door opens, and they see a walker, swung aside by the white-haired man in a gray polo shirt and white socks with sandals. His pale skinny knees poke out from under plaid shorts. "Please sit down. This can't be good news." He waves them to the sofa and sits in a lift chair that gently lowers him.

"It's not. I'm sorry to tell you that Mom died Thursday night, peacefully in her sleep." The old man gasps, removes his glasses, and pinches the skin between his eyes. "Thursday night, you say?"

"Yes. I'm sorry you had to hear a couple days after the fact," Dante says. "It was a shock to us and so much to do suddenly. I've always heard about people dying peacefully in their sleep but never known it to happen. And we knew you'd be expecting her to come."

Dante had once read that dying "peacefully during sleep" is improbable. They might have been having a terrible nightmare or been awakened by a failure of heart or lungs. At home, lacking professional care monitors, no one really would know the exact cause of death. And an autopsy is unnecessary, as are those facts. Dante hopes that Mr. Bisignano can take some comfort from a peaceful death; accuracy is not important.

"I thought it would be me first. Hoped it would." He shudders, trying to recover. "Is the funeral planned?"

"The burial plot's in New Hampshire, so we're taking her ashes there for a funeral Mass in the old parish in the spring." Then Dante suddenly adds, "We'll have a Mass said for her here, too, whenever you'd like."

"Can I get you a glass of water, Mr. Bisignano?" Cecilia says, standing up, frightened for him.

"Yes, thank you." Staring at the floor, he seems to be trying to grasp this massive loss. Straightening up, as if suddenly remembering his company, he says, "Angelina and I both had happy marriages. We talked about our former spouses a lot. You'd be surprised how many good things I know about your dad. When we met, it was a gift. Old people so miss that companionship, a simple touch means so much."

Cecilia hears this coming back into the room and hands him the water, with obvious relief.

"Take your time, Mr. Bisignano," she says.

He sips, then says. "At night, we said the prayer from the *Book of Numbers*:

'The Lord bless you and keep you.

The Lord let his face shine upon you, and be gracious to you.

The Lord look upon you kindly and give you peace.'"

With tears now streaming down her face, Cecilia reaches into the Kleenex box by Mr. Bisignano's chair and hands Dante one, seeing his eyes well up. She uses one to pat her own eye.

Dante realizes that nighttime prayer must be a part of the funeral Mass. Both masses. "My daughter Joan called the church to get your contact information," he says. "That's when we learned—did you know we thought you were a woman friend named Frances? That we thought you and she made biscotti all these years?"

"Well, I'm not surprised. Angelina was firm that we not meet."

"Why? We're so puzzled. It seems so unlike her. We can't fathom any reason," Dante says.

"You're the reason, Dante," he said, his voice cracking. "Why?"

Il Malocchio, Mr. Bisignano thinks. The Evil Eye upon her sons. "Since you were widowed, she's prayed for another good woman for you. She was busy with your family, so once a week was fine with me." He thinks of Nick's wife, Collerico, the hot-headed woman. "Then your brother's divorce made her wish the same for him. She felt a bit guilty—I guess you'd say—about our happiness."

Dante sits, distraught. For once not knowing what to say. He removes his glasses to wipe his eyes.

"Do you have any children nearby?" Cecilia asks. "We don't want to leave you alone now."

"My son and grandson are in North Port. I'll call Paul." He looks at his landline.

"May we have your number, Mr. Bisignano? We'll want to call to be sure you reached him," she says.

Cecilia sees a pad by the phone and tears off a sheet for him to write his number. Then says, "I'm going to leave you my number and Dad's. We want to keep in touch with you if that's OK." As they get up to leave, Mr. Bisignano pulls a lever, and the chair stands him up. He pulls the walker along, to accompany them to the door.

"I'm sorry Mom felt that way—letting us think you were a woman friend named Frances. I think we were deprived of getting to know you. I'm grateful for all you meant to her, Mr. Bisignano." Dante says, extending his hand.

The old man grasps with both of his, saying, "May I be perfectly Frank with you?" They all laugh through their tears.

"May I give you a hug?" Cecilia asks. Hugging him, Cecilia notes how short he is next to her 5'10". Nani had always been the shortest one. *Now I've become the smallest person in the family. But I'm way taller than Frank. Who Nani has somehow put into our family.*

"Your Nani thought the sun rose and set on you, Cecilia. You've got her big heart," Frank said as they broke away.

Cecilia offers to drive. Dad seems hit hard. Stunned he was by the reason for Nani's secrecy. As if she didn't deserve a turn at happiness because her son—in her opinion—didn't have it. *I've never thought of Dad as unhappy. Dad was still grieving when Nani moved in with us—we all were for a long time. But why hide Frank all these years later?*

"Cecilia, thank you for all you did," Dante says. "You were just what poor Frank needed, and he's obviously grateful. I am too. I'm so relieved you came along. I'm still…" He waves a hand, not knowing how to finish saying what—? *Overcome? Confused? Feeling guilty Mom had to hide her own happiness from me?*

"Dad, I've wondered—and I think Joan has too—why haven't you found a woman in all these years? We know you've dated. Sometimes stayed out all night—with Nani playing along." She pulls into the driveway, turns off the motor, and they stay in the car. "Why, in all these years, haven't we ever met any of those women?"

"There's never been one worth bringing into the family. No one on the level of the mother you lost," Dante says.

Silence. Cecilia asks, "Do you believe in heaven?"

"Yes," Dante says. "I don't believe in much. But the greatest man who ever lived referred to heaven twice in the short prayer he taught us. Whatever it is—some plane of existence after death—I don't know. I still offer up thoughts—words—to your mom. Usually at night before sleep. Sometimes in the daytime when something makes me think of what she'd say or think."

"So can jealousy exist there—wherever she is?"

"No. Envy's one of the Seven Deadly Sins. Can't be in whatever heaven is."

"So Mom would never envy a woman that you find. In heaven, Mom wants your happiness here. And now. Just as Nani did and does. And I hope you know that Joan and I do too."

"I've never thought of all the women in my life as judges on such a matter," Dante says, smiling. "But yes, I'd agree with all you're saying. I'm not *not* wanting to find someone. It's just not easy."

"Tell me about it!" Cecilia says sarcastically, getting out of the car. Dante comes around to her side and gives her a bear hug. "Thank you. What would I ever do without you?" Cecilia feels a swell of gratitude, feeling that Dad's words about such a vital place for her in the family are the most hopeful she's ever heard. Given in the midst of their grief.

They pick up Frank to come watch TV on Friday evenings now. Nani's old recliner is the only one that can lift Frank up to a full standing position when he wants to get out, so he sits in her chair. Dante's glad it's there now, recalling when Nani's heavy furniture from "up north" turned Lilliana's once light-and-breezy Florida room into an odd mix of light-and-sturdy that now provides everyone comfort.

Trump has quit *The Celebrity Apprentice* to run for president, and they've switched to *Shark Tank*—a favorite show of entrepreneurs and wannabes. Frank's a retired firefighter, who always had a second job, as did most firefighters. His gig work was on a printing press in his basement. Before home computers and printing/shipping stores, Frank was his town's go-to guy for invitations, fliers, any printed handout.

"I get a kick out of Mr. Wonderful," Frank says. "Kevin O'Leary plays the nasty Shark, but he's got moxie. Knows his stuff and can laugh at himself."

"I like Lori," Joan says. "She's often the only one seeing promise in a way-out presentation. Remember the Squatty Potty guy? He sat—fully clothed—to show his slanting toilet stool, claiming it's the best way to go." They laugh. "But Lori got the anatomy pitch. That potty's the show's most lucrative product of all. Sells well at Ace!"

"OK, I gotta give a shout-out to Mark Cuban, the Dallas Cowboy guy," Cecilia says, raising her glass. "The only billionaire Shark. The others only own hundreds of millions." *He's also a Libertarian, but we don't talk politics.*

"Mavericks," Joan says. "He owns the Mavericks—basketball, not baseball." Cecilia makes a "whatever" eye roll.

Frank laughs. "That exchange between you girls reminds me of a story Angelina told me of when you were little tots. Cecilia, she said you were slow to talk—as second children often are—letting an older child speak for them. Sometimes you'd just mutter toddler gibberish, and she'd ask 'Joan, what does Cecilia want?' And you'd tell her. One day after your gibberish, she asked you what Cecilia said, and you were quiet for a minute. Then you said, 'I think she's speaking Spanish.' Your playmate's grandmother spoke Spanish in their home, and you thought Spanish meant whatever you can't understand."

"Your Nani loved that story," Dante says and thinks, *Yiddish. It was Yiddish they spoke. Good story either way. Mom would have heard it from Lilliana.*

They quietly enjoy Nani's tale from beyond the grave, moved by the power of family stories, retold throughout the years, linking generations to one another, as the storyteller changes—and often even the story changes. Frank has become important to all of them.

As Joan and Dante are cleaning up pizza boxes to get ready for the program, Frank asks Cecilia, "Your dad tells me you're moving: where? And when?"

Cecilia freezes for a minute. "Well, my plans are kinda unsettled still. Pretty much up in the air now. Trying to size up my options. Lots going on."

Frank looks puzzled, sensing this isn't a welcome topic. Black sharks are swimming in the blue ocean as the show begins, and they're all immediately drawn to the TV.

Joan glances at Cecilia, knowing how she's struggling. *The first thing she told me about Barry is that his father died when he was nine. Meaning: he knows what we learned so young after a parent's death. Later she told me his dad's heritage was Irish-German—his mom's Dominican and—most importantly—she and Barry love talking politics!*

She doesn't earn enough to rent an apartment in Sarasota, and he's invited her to move to DC. But marriage isn't on the table, and she's starting to hear the biological clock ticking. Plus, starting over in DC would be even more financially challenging. Cecilia was speaking Spanish.

11
Free Choice/May 2017

Driving Frank home from one of their pizza/*Shark Tank* get-togethers, Cecilia tells him she's disappointed to learn that Mark Cuban is a fan of Ayn Rand's *The Fountainhead*. "He claims to have read it three times—a novel where a woman falls in love with—and marries—her rapist."

"Good heavens," Frank says. "Well, Rand goes way back to the 1940s, long before the women's rights movement. People were naive about portraying that kind of thing then—obviously even women writers. She probably saw a kind of *Gone with the Wind* episode—a dashing Clark Gable carrying a struggling Scarlett upstairs. It seems peculiar now that folks once showed that as manly, rather than violent."

"Yes, but Mark Cuban lives in *this* era," Cecilia says.

"True, but given who Cuban is, he probably focused on other parts, not the *amore bello*. And Rand was all about free choice—having your own business—doing it your way. You know, since Angelina died, I've been re-reading old novels that I'd loved well enough to keep for decades. What's surprised me is how much differently I now view so many novels I once loved."

Then he asks, "Do you know the librarian's rule for how long you should read a novel before you give up on it?"

Cecilia indicates no.

"Subtract your age from one hundred—stick with that many pages before giving up. So I don't give any of them more than twenty pages if it isn't compelling. I have too little time and there's too many good books out there!" They laugh, and Frank says, "The librarian adds, 'After age one hundred, you can judge a book by its cover!'"

"Why do you think your taste in novels changed so much?" Cecilia asks.

"Well, I have to care enough about some character—want to find out what happens to him or her. I don't engage with some characters at this age and stage of life as I once did. The Frank who read those books in his twenties and thirties is in the past. In my eighties, I find myself often fascinated by different characters and situations."

"Do you think that applies to people too?" Cecilia asks. "Would you fall in love with a different type of person now than you did in your twenties?" She pulls into Frank's driveway and turns off the engine.

"Interesting question! I loved two different women, very different ladies, you might say. But both were kind. Both smart. Both fun and funny. Both shared my values. I think Margaret and Angelina would have liked one another," Frank says.

"But since half of marriages end in divorce, I wonder if I wait longer to get married would I be attracted to a different guy."

"You're thinking about marriage now?"

"Yeah. Barry needs to spend full-time in DC. He'd like me to come with him. But it's like No Marriage is a policy of his. I want to have children someday and want marriage when I'm ready for that. Guys feel they have all the time in the world—'cause they do! Plus—I'd have to start all over to find work in a strange city."

"Major decisions, I can see."

"And they're terrifying! What if I go there and can't find enough work? And miss all I have back here?"

Cecilia turns to face Frank, and almost whispers: "What do you think Nani would say?"

Mamma Mia! Frank thinks, looking out the windshield into the dark. "I think she'd ask: 'Do you love him?'"

"If I said, 'I think so,' what would Nani say to that?"

Silence. Frank turns to look at Cecilia and says, "I think she'd ask—can you live with fear and possible failure if you go to DC? Or, can you live with safety and possible regret if you stay here?"

Looking surprised, Cecilia stiffens her back, then exhales, seemingly composed. *I don't want to live with regret.* Turning to him, she says, "I'm so glad you're with us now, Frank. We both miss her dreadfully, but I always feel she's with us when we're together."

"Me too, my dear. I'm sure she is." He removes his safety belt as she unlatches the trunk to get his walker. At the front door, when he turns to give her a hug, Cecilia asks "Do you think you know what Nani would expect me to choose?"

"Yep!" Frank says, chuckling and nodding. "I have a hunch, I do." *Chi non fa, nonfalla.* Those who do nothing, achieve and learn nothing.

From the window, he watches Cecilia get back in the car, then turns off his porch light, thinking: *Go for it, Cecilia. If it doesn't work out: 'chiodo scaccia chiodo'. You'll get over it.*

Once home, Cecilia goes to Wikipedia to search for Mary Matalin to see if she's still married to Carville. *Yeah. And Matalin has just become a Libertarian!*

###

October

TO: CeciliaPR@gmail.com
FROM: JoanAceHW@srq.com
SUBJECT: Desperation

I miss you so much. So I've started online dating.

TO: JoanAceHW@srq.com
FROM: CeciliaPR@gmail.com
SUBJECT: ?

How's that going?

TO: CecililaPR@gmail.com
FROM: JoanAceHW@srq.com
SUBJECT: What's out there

Makes me miss you even more! Guys lie about their height, age, marital status. I've had two wearing no wedding ring, claiming to be divorced—when Facebook page showed otherwise!

Even separated-but-not-divorced online guys are shopping for a mate before their divorce is final, or even initiated. Men way more reluctant than women to live alone.

TO: JoanAceHW@srq.com
FROM CeciliaPR@gmail.com

Cuz the women in their lives do all the housework, cooking, childcare & hold down a job.

TO: CeciliaPR@gmail.com
FROM: JoanAceHW@srq.com
SUBJECT: Men living mother-to-wife

now wanting a BETTER wife! And quite a few guys drink more than I want to be with.

I'm finding out what Dad's finding out about online dating. Except I'm not getting the funny stories Dad tells.

TO: JoanAceHW@srq.com
FROM: CeciliaPR@gmail.com
SUBECT: And yet…

Yet most people meet their spouses online. There's the possibility of a great match out there. Why not set a deadline—timewise/datewise? As you learn to navigate the swamp. And/or get a puppy (maybe)?

12

Bed Bugs and Love Bugs/2018

Just back from allergy tests, Nick texts Dante.

TO: DanteAceHW@srq.com
FROM: NickAceHW@srq.com
SUBJECT: bed bugs

I'm allergic to only one thing: bed bugs! I've been taking Claritin, watching pollen count, assuming it was something outdoors. NOT! It's inside—critters—in my bed. Dr. says it's either a serious infestation or I'm hyperallergic to them. Or both. Says it's not the bug itself, but their poop that people are allergic to.

TO: NickAceHW@srq.com
FROM: DanteAceHW@srq.com
SUBJECT: Aaargh!

Disgusting!

TO: DanteAceHW@srq.com
FROM: NickAceHW@srq.com
SUBJECT: Questions

"Now do I buy a new mattress?
Boil my sheets?
Find 'Tide for Bed Bugs'?"

TO: NickAceHW@srq.com
FROM: DanteAceHW@srq.com
SUBJECT: Get an exterminator

This is beyond DIY bug spray. Ask him about your situation. Get a quote.

The next day, Nick decides to tackle other pests while waiting for his appointment with exterminator Liberty Garcia. It's love-bug season, and the grill of his Cardinal Red Metallic: Mercedes Maybach SUV is plastered with these gooey black bugs. The often-recommended wet dryer sheets are doing the job on his car.

He's more disturbed that the home that's been his solace is infested with something worse than these sticky pests. He's made this post-divorce fixer-upper into his sanctuary. He didn't realize how Rosemary had exhausted him until he got this place. The luxury of peace and quiet. A great spare bedroom for the grandkids' visits.

Having seen how daughter Tracy has influenced her brothers' choices of wives, Nick thinks, *If I'd had a sister, I probably wouldn't have married Rosemary. In high school, I was attracted to what I saw as Rosie's spark, not realizing it was more of an assault weapon.*

He recalls her last tirade in their marriage, in a cafe— leading to being asked to leave, then on the drive home, telling Rosemary that her demands had been outrageous.

"I'd rather be outrageous than invisible!" Rosemary shrieked, seeing only two choices. Both extremes. No middle road.

And what the hell is a life coach—which she claims to be now?

Coaching reminds him of his days as the kids' baseball coach. *Loved coaching the kids. I'm at my best in teamwork. Dante and I are a good team. I'd like a partner at home too. I've come to feel…underutilized.*

Nick shuts the two cats in his garage. The exterminator's bringing a bedbug-sniffing dog. *Who knew?* He dumps his sack of soiled dryer sheets into the trash, checks his phone, and sees that it's time for the "bed bug control and prevention expert."

When Liberty meets a girl in a bar and she asks what he does, does he say he's a bed bug control expert? Obviously very employable in Florida. Siri tells Nick that, once eradicated in America, bed bugs returned with a vengeance after DDT was banished. *Liberty and his dog will provide my "free" bed bug inspection, which will end with the firm's "Year-Round Protection Plan." No doubt renewable. Forever.*

As a white Chevy Volt enters his driveway, Nick thinks *electric hybrid*, then is surprised as the door opens to see that the control/prevention expert Liberty is a woman. He notes a familiar college insignia on her license plate holder. She gets out of the car and says, "Hello, you must be Mr. Moretti. I'm Liberty." Letting a golden Labrador out of the back, "And this is Daisy, my partner."

"And I'm Nick, and"—pointing to her license frame—"Is that a Wildcat?"

"Yes. You're from New Hampshire too?"

"Yeah. Been in Sarasota a long time now. But still follow the Wildcats."

"Go Cats! I was a drummer!" Liberty says.

"There aren't many of us in Sarasota," Nick says. "My brother's here and some of our kids. But we're a distinct minority." Opening his front door, "Come on in."

Once inside, Liberty says "We'll get right to work if that's OK with you."

"Sure. I'll be in the kitchen," he says. "After I see just how your teamwork functions. I'm curious!"

"By all means," Liberty says. "We'll start in the living room here." He stands at the threshold, watching. Liberty point to a wall socket. Daisy sniffs, then stands, waiting. This happens a few times until Liberty points to a lounge chair: Daisy sniffs, then sits. Liberty gives her a treat. "She's indicating bugs in your chair," Liberty says, pointing to the sofa. Daisy sniffs and sits again. "And the sofa." This time Daisy's treat is a toy, and they play for a minute.

Nick groans. "I thought bedbugs were just in beds. By definition."

"They like to hide wherever humans recline. Then they can occupy other areas too."

"OK. I'll leave you to it," Nick says. Stretching his arm toward the stairway, he points upward—"And there's three bedrooms upstairs."

Horrified at bedbugs in his lounge chair and sofa, Nick is yet in awe of this teamwork. *Amazing!* Sitting at the kitchen table with a mug of coffee while they search upstairs, Nick frets that bedbugs might suggest a lack of cleanliness. He hasn't wanted to deal with his housecleaner, Hannah.

She runs the ceiling fans on high when she works—trying to cover her smoking—and usually forgets to turn them off. *I furnish No-Scent floor cleaner and other Ace cleaning products, but when I get home the cigarette smoke mingles with some kind of spray stuff. Open my door to an overwhelming stench of coconut cigarette smoke—smells like every grungy Miami cab I've ever taken. Does she think that odor signals "clean"?*

He knows that she hates cats. *They're terrified of the vacuum so would stay out of her way. But she obviously shuts them in the downstairs bathroom. When she cleans that bathroom, she leaves the vacuum out in the living room to keep them out of there—cats afraid of it even when it's off. So they hide in the kitchen. Last week I came home to this "cleaned house" to find a vomited hairball on the kitchen floor.*

Nick's annoyance at Hannah is reduced to: Will Liberty think my home is unclean? This seems worse than he'd imagine it could be.

When they return, Nick asks, "Will I have to get rid of all this padded furniture?"

"No. We'll work with heat treatments, ideally soon—while we're still having cooler weather. Heat eliminates bugs at all life stages and should prevent future infestations. And it's environmentally friendly." Her tone is reassuring. "This isn't unusual in Florida. I've seen far worse. You have a lovely home, and we'll make it perfect again."

Nick checks her finger. No wedding ring. "Have a chair," he says, pointing to the one across from him. His glasses slip down Nick's Roman nose that Dad called "our beak," and he pushes them up with an index finger while standing to ask, "Can I offer you a cup of coffee while we discuss your plan?"

"Sounds great," Liberty says, sitting, then settling Daisy on the floor beside her chair. "First, do you have questions?"

"Yes. Where are you from in the Granite State?" he asks, setting her coffee cup on the table.

She laughs. "I was in college at Durham. My family farmed in Merrimack County."

"What did you study at UNH?"

"Funny you should ask," she says. "I first got intrigued with invasive species there. Aquatic and domestic. My degree work was interrupted with marriage, having two children, and divorce. But I'm still chasing invasive species. Where are you from?"

"Laconia."

"Ah. Beautiful town."

"True. But I don't miss winters." He sets a small tray with sugar and creamer and pours the coffee. "Final question: why did your parents name you Liberty?"

"They were Peter Pans—kids who came over from Cuba when Castro got into power—in the early '60s. Everyone thought he'd be out in a few months. Wrong by half a century and more!"

Liberty takes out paperwork and asks, "Do you live alone here?"

"Yes, unless you count Fred and Ginger, my cats."

She puts down her tablet to look at him. "A cat man? Do you dislike dogs?"

"No, they're just too much work. I love the self-reliance of cats. And they're very clever."

"Daisy and I could debate you about the cleverness of dogs versus cats."

"Oh, I see you could. Obviously. Daisy holds down a job! Tell her I'm not a species bigot. Dogs are more trainable and useful, and she really is a beauty. I've been wondering: what stops her from falsely indicating bugs to get a treat?"

"Teamwork. Some dogs do have a tendency to give a false signal, so you have to work to eliminate that." Liberty says. "My part is to accurately indicate the search spot, so I don't accidentally give a false cue. Daisy has been a marvel to train and work with."

"I assume Daisy lives with you, that you own her?" Nick asks.

"Yes, we're a forever team. What is your work schedule like? I want to send you a proposal."

"I'm self-employed, so free to arrange my work schedule. Doing it before the weather gets hot sounds perfect."

"Good. Just let me know if you have any questions. I'll give this priority."

"Your New Hampshire roots seem to have influenced your pest-free career—reflecting our state's motto: 'Live Free or Die'," Nick says, hand over heart.

Liberty raises an eyebrow, smiling. "As long as you don't take me for granite. Please call me Libby."

He escorts her to the door, wondering: *Was she flirting with me?* "I look forward to seeing you again," he says, smiling.

"You'll hear from us soon," she tells him, patting Daisy's head. Nick shuts the door. Makes a fist pump, then stands with his hands tucked under his armpits, savoring the moment, before walking to the garage door.

Saying, "Hey, kitties," Nick opens the door to welcome Fred and Ginger back inside.

###

Liberty settles Daisy in the back. "Good girl, you did so well." She gets into the car and backs out of the driveway onto the street, thinking of the house they just worked. Exquisite furnishings with hickory floors throughout, real wood. Nice bisque-colored walls, accent pieces in turquoise, sea foam green, royal blue. Chocolate leather sleeper chair. Peaceful. Washing machine open; he uses it as a laundry basket and sets on cold to wash all colors together.

Spare bedroom for kids with twin trundle beds low to the ground, lots of pillows, all encased in a big tent. Kids love a fort, and this one's to sleep in. No bugs in the kids' room or his office, with its beautiful bookcases. Cherry wood?

"He's got great taste," she tells Daisy, "And yet, that lovely home lacks a little something: plants, a throw blanket, placemats. Especially plants." Pulling up for a red light, she looks at the dog in the mirror. "It could use a woman's touch, couldn't it, girl?" Daisy looks up, hoping for a treat.

###

TO: CeciliaPR@gmail.com
FROM: JoanAceHW@srq.com
SUBJECT: Sisters

I'm still your big sister & now a Big Sister. Vera Osorio, 16. Lives in Manatee County. Customer asked to put fliers @ cash register re. the need—esp. for teenagers. Scary-challenging (for those of us who never had kids!) Decided to plunge in.

TO: JoanAceHW@srq.com
FROM: CeciliaPR@gmail.com
SUBJECT: Great news!

Fabulous! What's she like? What do you two do together?

TO: CeciliaPR@gmail.com
FROM: JoanAceHW@srq.com
SUBJECT: Vera

She's shy, lonely (I'm lonely too since you left.) First meetings a bit awkward, but her mom's appreciative & encouraging. So muddling through, getting acquainted. It's kinda DIY. Trying to come up with what works.

So far best outing going to Ace. She asked where I work & when I told her said she's never been in a hardware store!

TO: JoanAceHW@srq.com
FROMCeciliaPR@gmail.com
SUBJECT: !!
What does she like so much about it?

TO: CeciliaPR@gmail.com
FROM: JoanAceHW@srq.com

Everything! It's her Disneyland! I let her pick out things to take home. Cherished items: Sani-Sticks drain pipe cleaner (all their drains slow); Swifter Extender Duster (to tackle cobwebs @ corners of ceilings); plastic drawer organizers; shower caddy, Apricot BBQ Sauce—sounded good to her though she'd never heard of it, or any of the products. Ace was our great adventure. I'll bring her back seasonally, as we change inventory.

TO: JoanAceHW@srq.com
FROM: CeciliaPR@gmail.com
SUBJECT: Vera's so fortunate

You're the best sister ever.

A Mating Man-Plan

Nick has come to Dante's house for dinner and to look at some of their mother's belongings.

Nick sits at the kitchen table, while Dante digs into the freezer, pulling apart some Healthy Choice bowls, asking: "Spicy Black Bean & Chicken or Basil Pesto Chicken?"

"I don't care, you pick. Don't you ever get tired of those frozen bowls?"

"The ease of them never wears off. Not having to think about making dinner." Dante puts one in the microwave and punches the time. "Though I miss Mom's cooking every time I sit down to eat." A *ding* has him opening the door, and he peels the film from the top of that bowl while walking over to set it down in front of Nick. "Go ahead, while it's hot."

After punching in his own bowl's minutes, he pours a Miglianico Montepulciano into two glasses, raises his and says, "*Cin cin.*"

While his bowl is spinning, Dante walks into the dining room and picks up two well-worn books and brings them to the table. After the *ding*, he removes his own bowl dinner and sits in the other chair. Nick recognizes the old books. "Wow. It's been a few years since we read these!" he says, separating them on the table. "Mom's Italian *Pinocchio*, and the one we wanted—in English!"

"You've got grandchildren at the right age, so you get the English," Dante says. "Mom was reading the Italian one to me around the time of my First Confession."

"It was so pertinent to me—that story of a puppet wanting to have a conscience so he could be a real boy! Wait, wasn't it Geppetto who wanted Pinocchio to be a real boy?"

"No, no, that was the movie! Disney changed the story and lost the point—which is why Mom wouldn't let us see the movie."

"Though I saw it during an overnight at Jimmy Benfari's house," Nick says, laughing. "What was so wrong about it?"

"The book's Pinocchio is a darker dude. Written by a seminarian, Carlo Collodi—back in the 1800s. His puppet is so hardhearted he allows Geppetto to be jailed for his own bad deeds. When his conscience first appears—as a cricket—that Pinocchio kills it. It appears afterward only as a ghost. In the movie, it's the puppet's bad companions that drive Jiminy Cricket away."

"Does all that really matter?"

"It matters because Disney's puppet is just naive, so he lacks the one thing necessary for a conscience—culpability. That's the whole point of the story—and of First Confession's practice of examining your conscience!"

"You took everything so seriously then," Nick says, smiling. "I don't recall agonizing about my own First Confession."

"It was serious to me, but it wasn't agony. It was a delight; I loved that story about doing good in the world. Collodi's Pinocchio begins to suffer the consequences of his terrible behavior, and he himself starts longing to become a real boy. He becomes a flesh-and-blood son only after he allows his conscience to transform him into a loving child."

"Wow. I've always kinda thought of conscience as a mother-in-law who comes to visit—and never goes back home." They both laugh, thinking of Nick's former mother-in-law, Matilde, a humorless woman who always had a complaint.

"So do you still think of conscience as Jiminy Cricket?" Nick asks, smiling.

"Well, I think of it as the ghost of my better self," Dante says, getting up to turn on the coffeemaker and bring a plate of biscotti to the table. "We're gonna miss Mom. She was the heart of the family."

"Are you going to stay here in this big house now, alone?"

Dante pours a second glass for both of them and says, "No. Too much upkeep, so I'll start looking for something else. I'm not sure what I should get."

"Nothing positive yet from the online dating?"

Dante gives a thumbs down.

"What's your purpose with this online stuff?" Nick asks.

"To meet a pleasant person, with whom I'll ultimately become intimate, safely, sexually, with a long-term goal."

"You tell them you work at Ace, not that you own thirteen stores..." Nick, asking. Dante nods. "You've investigated arrest records?" Nick swings a finger in circles, indicating et cetera.

"That's a first step now," Dante says. "As Chief DiPino reminded me long ago, there are dangerous women out there."

"So conversation is trying to figure each other out? Convey what's important?"

"Ideally, the first date would reveal that. I'd like an honest question-answer exchange. No detail, no talking too long. See where that goes."

"Get to the heart of the matter," Nick says. "OK. I dare you to answer *every* question truthfully on your next date. And ask only what you really need to know to move beyond the first date. If you're hunting for a relationship, long-term, that's a start. Short and sweet—or bitter—results."

"You're on. I'll do it. I have a coffee date tomorrow morning," Dante says. "What about you, Romeo?"

"I'm seeing someone. Her name is Liberty."

"Whoa." Dante's surprised. "How'd you find Liberty?"

Nick grins. "I took your suggestion."

"To do what? When have *I* ever given you advice about meeting a good woman?"

"I'm in love with that exterminator you told me to hire!"

Coming Out

Dante's date this morning is Jan Whitney: fifty-two, divorced. Jan's profile suggests a serious woman with a long career as a Sarasota realtor. She looks pretty in a tropical print dress—having daughters makes him recognize it as a Lily Pulitzer.

Starbucks is his go-to meeting place. Jan was prompt, as he was, with no time to waste. No doubt she has a showing after this.

They both listen to and support classical music. They enjoy movies and Sarasota's live theater and are both avid readers. So far, so good. Her favorite authors—Jane Austen, Louise Penny, Fanny Flagg. *Never heard of the last one, but I'd expect gender preferences.* "I've been reading The Sermon on the Mount," he says.

Her eyebrows shoot up, and she reaches across the small table and puts her hand on top of his, saying, "Bless your heart. That should always help put our lives in perspective."

She had just returned from her native Charlotte, North Carolina, having indicated that something stressful occurred there.

"Has it been helping you right now?" Dante asks, acknowledging her earlier reference to just returning from a somewhat disappointing trip.

"It was a tough week. My daughter Brittany came out, and her dad of course had to be there. Tension all around!"

Came out gay? Or trans? Dante wonders. "Was your ex-husband on board?" he asks.

"Oh, he wanted to be in the limelight. To make it all about him."

"But Brittany has a good grasp on all that's involved?"

"Well, it's all over now."

"Brittany's had the surgery?"

"Surgery? It wasn't surgery!"

"Oh. She came out as gay?"

Jan stiffens her spine. "She came out in *society*. At the *Cotillion!*"

Surprised, Dante emits a "Haargh," trying to stifle laughter by blotting a napkin over his mouth. *She "came out" to DANCE?!*

"Sorry. I misunderstood that whole 'coming out' business." He doesn't sound sorry, his upper body shaking as he attempts—unsuccessfully—to suppress laughter. *Nick, where are you now?*

The blond guy at the nearby table notices Dante trying to stifle laughter as his lady companion seems enraged. His eyes meet Dante's, and he can't help but give a slight laugh at whatever's causing this awkward dilemma.

Furious now, Jan pushes her chair back and starts gathering her things. "My daughter's not a freak of nature! She's a proud new member of the United Daughters of the Confederacy!" Both guys at the next table can't help but overhear that.

Dante's eyes again meet the blond guy's as he thinks, *The Confederacy? Talk about a lost cause—it's gotta be this date!* Dante's uncontrollable giggling makes it all worse.

Jan stands upright: "*My* Bible tells me that we should stay the sex God created for us. If my daughter told me otherwise, I'd have marched her straight to conversion therapy."

Conversion therapy? Dante thinks: *Yes! Convert Brittany to the Union. Join the U. S. of A.!* He can't stop his laughter from erupting now. Both guys at the other table hear it all, as they stare with big eyes at each other.

Jan storms out, turning to shout as she goes through the door, "We obviously don't read the same Bible."

"Truer words were never spoken," Dante says to his neighbors, blotting his eyes with the napkin, still laughing.

"We wanna read the one *you've* been reading," the blond one says, and the men all laugh.

On his drive home, Dante looks forward to telling Nick just what speaking your mind can get you. Clarity. Efficiency. Quickest date ever—fifteen minutes tops. *Giggling fit like I haven't had since grammar school Masses with that bad-assed Sister Hildegard patrolling the aisle, armed with her ruler.*

He knows that this dating story will go over well on Friday night too, ending with that Harry-met-Sally comment from the next table. *Still, even fifteen minutes is too much. I'm done with online dating.*

13

A Free Lunch / Summer 2019

Monday is her day off, and she invariably comes to the Ace Hardware near the Orioles Stadium for her projects. Abigail Curtis is the most interesting customer he's ever met. Add intriguing. Some weeks ago, he first saw her in the aisle leaning over to search the low shelf of paint.

An enticing view of this attractive woman, with her blond ponytail sticking out the back of an orange baseball cap. Dante pegged her as older than his daughters and under his age. Her confident certainty in reviewing products suggests she was closer to his fifties than to the girls' twenties.

"May I be of any help to you?" he asked, at their first meeting. She straightened up and turned around, revealing a little black Oriole on the front of her cap. "I'm looking for the magnetic paint," she said.

"One of my favorite products. Not many people know about it, so it's just in our bigger stores. I can get it sent over here from another store."

"I love it! I magnetize the wall above my computer. So handy to be able to stick stuff you need but don't want taking up space on your desk. I'd like to order a can. Can I pick it up next Monday? That's my day off."

"Sure. Do you know that after you put four coats on you can cover that black paint with two coats of the room's wall color? The magnet still works, and no one else knows how that stuff stays up on the wall!"

"Cool. I didn't know that. Now I like it even better." Lovely smile. Dimples. Dante thinks: *You never see dimples anymore.*

###

Next Monday, when Dante rings up the magnetic paint purchase, he asks the usual "Are you an Ace Rewards customer?"

"I've been one forever. I come from Chicago, where you're always walking distance from an Ace Hardware, even downtown."

"That's where it all began, back in 1924."

"Really? I don't know the history, just that they've been there my entire life."

"We're global now—China, Dubai, over five thousand stores. The highest density of them, though, is in the Chicago area!"

"Looks like Sarasota's doing pretty well too. I see them up and down Tamiami Trail."

She wouldn't know my family owns them all. He says, "People come here and buy a home—first or second—and that leads them to us. Can I carry this out to the car for you?"

###

Dante's in that store every Monday now. He told employees he likes to keep in touch with shopper trends and changes in customer preferences. Manager Carlos wonders why he limits customer research to the smallest of his many stores. Eventually, Carlos—and the employees—notice that Dante's research centers on one customer. The crew notices when Abigail comes in: she's the one. Future Mondays have her buying insulation, drywall, joint compound. She knows all about whatever it is she's doing.

On another Monday, Dante says, "I'm curious about your projects. You seem to work awfully hard on your day off!"

"I'm building a tiny house."

"Really! I love that show on Home & Garden TV. How big?"

"Three-hundred-sixty square feet."

"Fascinating. What stage are you in now?"

"I'm doing the interior work now. I bought the basic structure from the Amish," she says.

"Next time you come in, bring photos, OK?"

After she left, Dante found Carlos in the lighting aisle, to tell him, "Our Monday customer—Abigail—is building a tiny house. Herself!" All the employees eventually get the news and agree that Abigail is their most interesting customer. Who wouldn't see his attraction? they say to one another.

###

On yet another Monday, Dante notes Abigail checking out 10/2 and 10/14 Romax wire, electronic staples, and wire connectors. "I see you're starting the wiring. Do you have a reliable electrician?" he asks.

"The best," Abigail says, smiling. "I do my own wiring."

Wow. Dante had never asked a customer out, nor been tempted to. No Ace Handbook on that. But there's no Ace Handbook on a woman who does her own wiring. Could asking her out risk making her so uncomfortable she'd start going to another Ace? (Or—god forbid—to Lowe's or Home Depot?) Still, he's eager to tell the staff that Abigail does her own wiring.

On the next Monday, Abigail pulls out her cell to show Dante a small trim cottage with tan vinyl siding and a red front door. She points to an outdoor overhang on one side. "You can make a patio under that, or screen it in for a porch, or use it to park a car."

"Fantastic. Had no idea the Amish built anything like this," Dante says, handing her phone back. "You have $40 in Ace Rewards. Do you want to take that on this purchase?"

"Please," Abigail says. "And I'd like to know if you're available someday to be my guest at lunch? Doesn't have to be a Monday."

Dante feels a rush. Surprise. Elation. "Sure. My schedule's flexible, so why don't you pick a day."

"Thursday OK? Any food allergies I should consider?"

"No, I eat everything," tapping his belly. "Unfortunately! Where would you like to meet?"

"How about Jack Dusty's?"

Restaurant at the Ritz Carlton. "Well, definitely I'd eat everything *there!*" Dress shirt and necktie Thursday. Ditch my red Ace shirt.

"I have to confess an ulterior motive."

"No-such-thing-as-a-free-lunch situation?" Dante asks, laughing and thinking, *What do I care?*

"Let me put it this way. I'm going to give you the opportunity to do a good deed," she says, gathering her bags.

Watching Abigail go out, Dante feels a quick fluttery rise in his chest. If he tried to put a name to it, he'd have to say hope.

Dante is glad it's Thursday, not a Monday, because Carlos and the others would see him in his best sports jacket and a tie and know of this…appointment, *whatever it is.* They're too involved on Mondays with Abigail. Their expectations can be a burden. *Managing my own is more than enough.*

He's been thinking all week about what to wear. Starting with what Joan gave him for his last birthday—the Zegna "exploded paisley tie" in many shades of blue with a bright orange background, which looked great on top of the bright white shirt in the box. Navy slacks. His bone-colored silk sport jacket.

This is the best I can look, Dante thinks, seeing himself in the mirror. Appreciating that Joan always shops at Saks for him. *Instead of where I order stuff—Land's End.*

Early, Dante sits in the Ritz lobby, waiting, wondering about Abigail's Good Deed. If she only knew! *She's got some favorite cause or charity she wants to involve me in. Our website shows I own Ace stores, so maybe wants a pledge. Or product donations. We do that for Habitat, so if that's it, this good deed doesn't count! Typical. But fine. We may share ideas about doing good in the world. No Daughter of the Confederacy here, I'll bet.*

A different, ready-for-business Abigail enters the Ritz. Dante sees her blond hair now freed from the baseball cap, *framing that beautiful face.* She's wearing a silver trench coat and red heels on this drizzly day. *Stunning.*

"You look lovely," he tells her.

"Thank you. You do too. We clean up well, don't we?"

The sun is starting to come out, and they agree to sit outside. She puts her briefcase in the empty chair and slips out of her silvery gray raincoat, which reveals a silky purple lining. She's wearing a crisp white blouse and dark gray slacks.

She urges Dante to order the cioppino (the most expensive dish on the lunch menu), saying she's going to order it too. "We can count it as our main meal of the day, so no worries about dinner. Your interest in my tiny house has led to this invitation. I'd like to tell you why I'm doing it."

"I'm eager to hear that."

"I'm heading an initiative to provide a few tiny houses for Sarasota street people," she says. "Those who are Veterans. I'm hoping the house I'm building will be a prototype for nine more. I can't build the rest of them myself, as I have a day job. But more on that later."

"I'm talking with the County about a parcel of land, near natural parkland, but close enough for access to the city. Veterans on the streets have some income but not enough to rent an apartment in Sarasota. Their benefits are enough to pay utility bills after they move in, and groceries—if they're not spending money on self-medication. I'm working with a Veterans' organization to determine which ones might be candidates."

"What you've just described—well it's an answer to a prayer in more ways than you could ever guess," Dante says. "I'm working with a homeless fellow right now with the help of the VA."

"Do you know Harold?—he's Vietnam. We've become friends."

"No, but what an amazing coincidence!" Abigail says, brightened with enthusiasm, and relief.

"How do you think I can help your little homes project?"

"Let's not get into that right now, because I had no idea you'd be able to see the vision so quickly. I want to hear more about Harold, and together we can talk about any involvement you'd like."

The waiter is placing big bowls of cioppino in front of each.

"Meanwhile, let's eat! Perhaps this calls for a glass of wine? Even mid-day?" Abigail asks.

"Only if you let me do that," Dante says, signaling the waiter to hand him the wine menu. She prefers white, and he orders an Italian pinot gris, at $30 a glass. *That better be the best wine we've ever tasted.*

"This is more celebratory than you can imagine," he says, as the wine is being poured.

"I'd like to tell you why." He raises his glass, and she clinks hers to it.

"Please do."

"Ten years ago, I went to confession. Hadn't been to confession for maybe twenty years. Got a third-world priest—the whole scene was new to me. The penance he gave me has been haunting me ever since."

"I can't wait…" She looks at him expectantly.

"He told me to do a good deed."

"Interesting. Why was that a problem? Isn't your work with Harold a good deed?"

"I'm the typical 'Helpful Ace Hardware man': I've been trying to find the good deed that I wouldn't have done anyway for ten years now. I'd taken other street people to a meal before him. I saw Harold walking across the Orange St. roundabout, jabbering on his cell, so distracted he'd have been killed if I hadn't rushed from behind, got out there, and put my hand up to stop cars. When he got to the curb, I introduced myself and told him that my wife had died doing that. Distractedly talking on her cell, she got hit by a car."

"I'm so sorry to hear that. What a shock that must have been."

"Our girls were ten and twelve." Dante sighs, then thinks, *Don't dwell there.*

"I took Harold to breakfast that day, and he told me of his service. He's a nice guy, PTSD, no surprises. I think he has great potential. But that was something I'd have done anyway. Which has been my long-time problem. Finding a good deed I *wouldn't* have done—as in this case—because

I wouldn't have known about it." He smiles, raising his glass to her. "Thank you, Abigail. I've finally found a true penance. And I couldn't be happier with it."

"I'd like to know more about this priest who gives someone who's been away from Confession for so long just one unspecified good deed. I wonder if they ever return to tell him what good deed they did. How would he ever know its effectiveness?"

"Well, he also told me to read The Sermon on the Mount, which I've been doing off and on too. Easy. I've enjoyed researching it."

"Do you remember Tip O'Neill—Speaker of the House in the 1980s?"

"Sure, a Bostonian. 'All politics is local'."

"He called The Sermon on the Mount the greatest political speech ever written."

"I've never heard that!" Dante says. "And I thought I'd read just about everything on that. Yeah: he would have meant the Beatitudes section of the Sermon. I love knowing that. This was an amazing lunch. Thank you."

When they leave, Dante walks her outdoors. A valet pulls up Abigail's black Volkswagen Passat and gives her the key. As Dante holds the door for Abigail to get in, he asks what he's wondered for some time: "By the way, what kind of work do you do on the other days? What's your regular job?"

"I'm an Episcopal priest," she says, fastening her seat belt while looking up at Dante's surprised face.

###

There is so much to be done for this endeavor with Abigail. A newly charged Dante has emerged. Enthusiastic. Creative. Grateful for the freedom to do good in the world. Energized by and with Abigail in a way he'd never expected to be again.

Lunch—and sometimes dinner—meetings are necessary. Over glasses of wine one evening, Abigail refers to his initial confession story.

"Many Christians feel there's no need for an intermediary for confession. During all that time, had it ever occurred to you to confess directly to God?"

"Catholics were once big on examination of conscience, recommended at the end of each day, though I don't know if many people practice it anymore. I did think a lot about how I need to shape up"—patting his belly—"physically and morally." She smiles.

"I had a good early confession experience, which I think led to my lifelong appreciation for interacting with a priest during confession. May I share it?" Dante asks.

"Of course, there's something compelling about confession stories."

"I was twelve. To examine your conscience before confession then, children would read the Ten Commandments—for help thinking of possible infractions. But they were no help with my awful sin. So I was stammering in the confessional. Didn't know how to get to it. My confessor realized I was struggling. He asked, 'Can you just say it in one word?'"

"'Doubt!' was the awful word!" He and Abigail laugh.

"And the priest said, 'Ahhh. Well, you must turn the burden of your doubt over to me. From this moment on, the full consequences of your doubt are on my shoulders. Just pray and continue to receive Communion, and it will be all right.'"

"A wise and humble man," Abigail says.

"Yes, and so unusual in that time for a priest to accept doubt—especially a child doubting! To acknowledge that it's a part of faith. Of any thinking person's beliefs of any kind, actually."

"He allowed curiosity, exploration. Which for you obviously—as a child—was to follow your nature."

"You've obviously thought lots about this stuff too. How did you come to be a priest?"

"Our denomination started ordaining women when I was growing up, so it was in the back of my mind," Abigail says.

"In college, I studied psychology and philosophy and married the year I graduated. After I discovered that my husband was cheating, I avoided having children, while trying to solve that problem—with counseling and therapy. I ended up concluding that was just his nature. Just who he is, a serial cheater."

"Some people do seem to have a knack and a propensity to cheat, I've found—in business, playing golf—when they think it suits them," Dante says.

"I came to feel that with cheaters in marriage, the secrecy—leading a double life—is part of the excitement. It's an addiction I hadn't known of—nor ever certainly met—before Rex."

"After the divorce, I entered Seminary and was eventually ordained. And here I am."

"I think I'd have been suspicious of anyone whose name was Rex," Dante says, elated that this jerk is history. They both laugh.

November

Joan picks up her "little sister" Vera at home, most often on a weekend. Home is a one-bedroom rental in a shabby two-story cinderblock apartment building in Bradenton, north of Sarasota. Vera abides by her mom's rule of never leaving the unit to go outside in the evenings. There have been incidents in the neighborhood involving drugs and guns. Vera's mom, Malena, is delighted to have Joan spending time with Vera, helping guide and strengthen what she's been trying to do alone. The father has never been in the picture.

Vera is a short plump girl, with a very limited—unflattering—wardrobe of T-shirts and jeans. Pulls her black hair carelessly into a ponytail, maybe just to get it out of her face. The makeup she wears doesn't help—too much on the eyes and an overly brownish-toned lipstick carelessly applied.

Vera sits slumped as if wanting to disappear. Joan has found that she'll talk about her teachers. She enjoys a biology class, which is into oceanography now. Loves singing in the school chorus. Her Spanish teacher is unable to handle the students at times and often yells at them.

Vera doesn't seem to know their relatives in Mexico. Never mentions friends.

What's worked best is a movie followed by dinner. Discussing the film while eating helps Joan feel they're getting to know one another, within this shy girl's comfort zone.

As a caregiver for elderly people, her mother, Malena, works a 3-to-11 shift Wednesday through Sunday—to get the $1.50 higher hourly rate. On weekend mornings, Vera walks to Sacred Heart Church, where she earns her own money by helping in the preschool classroom during Saturday and Sunday Masses. Vera gets a free lunch, as do most students at her high school. On her workdays, Malena leaves dinner in the refrigerator for Vera to reheat.

Malena has asked Joan to attend an evening Open House for Parents at the school, as she's never been able to go and would like to know Vera's teachers' views of her girl's work. It's still light at 7:00 p.m. when Joan pulls her car into the school's parking lot. She's welcomed at the entrance by the assistant principal, who hands her a sheet with teacher names and classroom numbers. Signage throughout the halls directs visitors to the open classrooms.

There aren't as many parents as this size school should warrant, Joan thinks, and she finds little waiting time in Vera's classrooms. She's eager to tell Malena that all her teachers speak well of Vera. She's saved Mr. Coleman—Vera's favored science teacher—for last. The sheet says he's also the boys' basketball coach.

The science classroom door is open, and a lanky African American man wearing a sport coat and colorful tie sits alone at his desk, reading a book. Hard to figure his age with that salt-and-pepper hair. Mostly pepper. As she enters the room, he looks up and stands, exhibiting a prominent Adam's apple. He removes his tortoiseshell reading glasses while putting down his book. Joan notices it's *The Good*

Lord Bird. As they shake hands he says, "Hello. I'm Parker Coleman, and you are…?"

"I'm Joan Moretti, here as Vera Osorio's Big Sister." Joan nods at the novel he's just put down, "I loved McBride's memoir—*The Color of Water*—which would be hard to beat. So, how's his fiction?"

"Fabulous," he says, laughing, motioning to the chair beside his desk. "Please have a seat. It's great that you're here for Vera. She's an outstanding student. Always on time, aces exams, enthusiastic about our ocean project. It's an honor to teach her and a pleasure to have her in my class."

"So glad to hear that, and not really surprised. Vera's mom will be thrilled too. Mrs. Osorio works nights and is a single mom, so…"

"Not unusual among our families. With all that kids today face that impedes their learning, I sometimes wonder if it's worth it to keep teaching. Then along comes a student like Vera, and I know I need to be here. Please tell Ms. Osorio that she's doing everything right. Vera is college material, and I hope to see her get in the right college when that time comes. And thank you for being her Big Sister. I know how valuable big sisters are because I have four of them!"

"Omigod!" Joan leans over laughing. "Isn't that Sister Overload? Too much of a good thing?"

"Not at all. Well, sometimes when we all lived at home—growing up—I felt they were a bit too advice-prone. But I always knew they had my back. Now they're a great blessing in my life, though we're spread all over the country at this point. We do family reunions every summer."

No other parents come, and they talk until it's time to close. Joan is thrilled with what she's learned from the attractive Mr. Coleman. N*o wedding ring.* When he stands to walk her out of his classroom, she notices he's wearing jeans and unusual boots. *Python!* she realizes. *An invasive species. How did he ever find them in his huge size?*

He offers to lend Joan his novel after he finishes it. She notes the word *lend.*

14
Harold Moves in
2020/First Quarter

For the small homes project, Dante and Nick have purchased four acres, which sit adjacent to a twenty-nine-acre Audubon Land Preserve in Manatee County. Nature lovers and bird watchers walk its trails. The community will be called St. Francis Gardens.

Ten homes are planned. Harold's is the first finished in Stage One of development, which will eventually be four homes—two on each side of a narrow, paved road. Each home will have a small yard, front and back.

Dante has found that managing this good deed properly could be a full-time job itself. He offers to sponsor hiring someone to oversee fundraising, coordinate the selection of candidates for home ownership, with the VA overseeing addiction and PTSD therapy, and coordinate Ace's donation of supplies to the site. Abigail is now hiring and directing workers to finish the interiors. Many are known, reliable Ace customers.

Sarasota Veterans helped them find Benaiah Jones, a leg amputee Iraq Veteran who got her college degree in communications on the GI Bill. She's now the project's new Corporate Responsibility Director.

In January, Ace stores face a run on face masks, as immigrants—first Chinese, then German and African—buy them to send to relatives abroad. A virus seems to be spreading from China into Europe and Africa. Construction workers who need these masks daily suddenly find empty shelves. Panic buying then moves to gloves and sanitary wipes. Craigslist sellers offer the items at a 170 percent markup of the Ace price.

Harold becomes the first St. Francis Gardens resident, as he moves into the unit that Abigail built. When Dante brings him a welcoming Ficus plant, Harold's eyes brim with tears, as he says, "You've saved my life twice now. I ain't gonna screw the pooch on this one, my friend."

He takes Dante on a tour of his three hundred sixty square feet of living space. They enter the living room. Its large double window lets in light that extends to the adjacent kitchen most of the day. He points out the microwave, toaster oven, two-burner cooktop, and a mini-refrigerator freezer. There's a small washer for clothes and a drying rack that can be used indoors or out. "I eat sitting at the counter on that stool," Harold says. Dante notes that Harold uses the kitchen table for some of his many projects.

Across from the kitchen is the bathroom, with a walk-in shower and storage closet, and he leads Dante down the other end to the bedroom. "I chose a single rather than double bed, which allows me that other closet in here," opening the door to show tools, bee-keeping paraphernalia he has started to collect, and his bike. "I like to keep my bike indoors because Florida humidity causes rust."

While waiting for neighboring units to be finished in March, Harold begins giving programs on bee hives for adults and children at the Preserve. He also becomes a one-man welcoming committee for each carefully selected new neighbor as other units get occupied, one by one. Harold's joy at using skills he'd forgotten—or didn't know he had—to help others strengthens him as well as them.

"Do you know there are places in China where the bees are gone now? They have to use paintbrushes to pollinate plants," Harold tells Dante. "Caring for these wild creatures, paying attention to them, listening to the colony, learning from them—it makes me look differently at just about everything now."

Harold tells his new neighbors that if a bee carries a lethal virus to the nest, his nest mates cut off the spread by building networks with different tasks. Some get food; some carry out waste. Those who are immune form a protective wall around the Queen. "And expecting this new coronavirus to contain itself without masking and social distancing is like roping off a section where you can pee in the swimming pool. This virus—like pee—doesn't stay where you want it to. We have to protect ourselves and one another."

Stage One's three other units are occupied as both Florida and New York announce their first virus cases. Epidemiologists advise Americans to wear masks and socially distance themselves, while President Trump claims the virus is "like the flu" and "will magically go away." But the VA—recalling the many soldiers killed during the WWI epidemic—warns of the dangers of close, unmasked confinement. Most Veterans are in the high-risk population now: older, with underlying conditions, predominately men—who are more vulnerable than women. Harold has told Dante and Abigail that each new neighbor's first two needs are sleep and water. Sleeping on the streets for so long leaves them arriving exhausted and dehydrated.

"They're not up to anything else until they can start to feel human again," he says.

Harold's experience with what each new resident is going through, and as a squad commander in Vietnam, along with his seniority as a resident, has him soon serving as president of the new Homeowners Association. In a timely manner, he communicates the rules for living together comfortably and securely and enforces the rules with the cooperation of his present and future neighbors.

The next pod of six homes—three on each side of the road—is underway. A resident meeting area and two picnic tables are planned for the open green space at the end of the road of houses. Harold is planting a garden, hoping to inspire his neighbors to do the same. "We can specialize in different vegetables, and share the bounty," he says. Abigail and Dante agree that Harold is the best possible resident to motivate his neighbors to cultivate beauty, goodwill, and pride in their tiny homes.

Governor DeSantis hasn't ordered a stay-at-home mandate, and Florida beaches and bars are packed with college kids on spring break—not wearing masks. Although Harold and his St. Francis Gardens neighbors occupy a sparsely populated parkland, Harold insists on socially distancing when together, easily done since they all ride to Publix and the city on bikes. It's not difficult to sit in a circle six feet apart on lawn chairs in the green space to talk in the evening, about how fortunate the timing of St. Francis Gardens has been for them. How terrible to be living on the streets now—with the libraries closed there's no place for street people to use a restroom.

By the end of March, much of the country is on lockdown. Nursing homes are overloaded with Covid-19 patients, as the virus also spreads through church services, weddings, and funerals. The President continues to contradict his own epidemic experts, and Americans are becoming divided about the use of lockdowns and social distancing to prevent contagion. Ace stores, including all the Morettis own, have remained open throughout, serving customers while maintaining all safety protocols.

TO: DANTEAceHW@srq.com
FROM: NickAceHW@srq.com
SUBJECT: 1Q

Can you believe this 1Q? Biggest 1Q gain in Ace 96-year history. People locked in, wanting to improve their property. Great to be open for them & our employees at work. We're luckier than most during this crazy time.

Vera's science teacher, Mr. Coleman, called to make arrangements to pass his novel to Joan right after the New Year before classes resumed. He was going to be in Sarasota so they met at a Panera, sitting outdoors. He says—credibly—that he's divorced, with two sons in the other Manatee high school. "This way they don't have me as a teacher or as a coach—where the other kids might suspect I favor them. I've coached my boys from Little League baseball, to basketball. Time to shift gears." The boys' mother attends their games, which usually coincide with Parker's teams' games.

They talk about parenting, with Joan confessing to being clueless most of the time. "With teenagers, we're all clueless most of the time," he says.

They talk about books recently read. They talk about their sisters, and Joan likes what she's hearing about his ties to family. Joan allows herself to become hopeful.

15

Courting in a Pandemic/ Second Quarter

Dante and Nick are having a beer on Nick's patio on a Saturday afternoon.

"Great text from Harold yesterday," Dante says. "Central Florida researchers he's in contact with notified him about an ultra-rare bee last seen in 2016, now in the St. Francis Gardens neighborhood. It's a metallic blue! Collects pollen only on its face, so has these unusual looking facial hairs—"

"Does anyone but Harold have a basis of comparison for facial hairs on bees?" Nick laughs.

"Nope! And Harold says this little sucker relies on a threatened plant that only flowers around Lake Wales in central Florida. He can't wait to get up there after the quarantine."

"He's still off booze and doing well with PTSD treatment?" Nick asks.

"Yep. In fact, He's inspired me; I've officially and finally quit smoking." Dante says. "All year I'd been trying to reduce how many I'd get a day. But all I thought of was my waiting for my daily smokes—my third, my fourth. Harold pointed out that what you fear is that terrible need for a cigarette, but that craving lasts less than thirty seconds. So I figure I can stand anything for thirty seconds, even if it happens every five minutes. And I don't think about them nearly as much now."

"My stationary bike at home now is easier than going out, and I've lost twenty-five pounds." Dante pats his slimmer belly. "Nothing else to do at home but get fit."

"I'm guessing your inspiration for all this is Father Abigail, right?" Nick asks. "That you've got the hots for a lady priest."

"They don't call women priests 'Father'—as you know. But get real: she's way out of my league. Hell, she's out of my entire universe. This woman deserves a leading man, not me. I'm just the best friend. The George Costanza."

"George is way too short to be you," Nick says. "You're more Larry David's best friend—Jeff Garlin. Big Guy. But Dante, c'mon. You're saying you've got the yips with *dating*? Like that Cubs pitcher who couldn't throw to first base? Lester—that zillion-dollar World Series pitcher with the heebie-jeebies who couldn't 'THROW THE BALL TO FIRST BASE'? My big bro has the dating yips?"

"No, no. You exaggerate. Besides—didn't Lester pitch the game that won the World Series for the Cubs after a hundred and eight years? In spite of his yips?"

"Yeah, but you don't have a hundred years. Why so pessimistic? What's the stance on an Episcopal divorced priest marrying a Cafeteria Catholic, anyway?"

"You're way ahead of me with those questions," Dante says.

"How do Joan and Cecilia ring in on this?" Nick asks.

"Well, I haven't discussed Abigail with them, other than her role heading the tiny house project. They don't know how much time we're spending together other than with St. Francis Gardens work."

"You're pulling *Mom's* secrecy stunt? Why?"

"No, no. I'm not lying about anything. But why get into that, anyway, with the girls when I don't know myself what to make of our relationship?"

"What do you want to happen?" Nick asks.

"I'd like to talk to the girls about marrying Abigail, in time. But I don't want to assume anything. Having her in my life in whatever works is what's important now. I'm not ready to risk pushing things."

"You gotta man up, bro. Set a target date. Or a target weight! Whatever. Move it along."

"Ha! I want to marry her, and I've never even kissed her. And now we're wearing masks! You can't rush this stuff in a pandemic."

"Noted," Nick says. "Speaking of which: didja see the Cuomo brothers on CNN last night?"

"Yeah," Dante says. "And we also got Fauci directing things now. Just heard recently of a vaccine research team in Pittsburgh, Dr. Starzi and Dr. Falo, working on a vaccine you'd apply like a band-aid. And a goombuddy named Gambotto—doing vaccine research in Italy for twenty-five years—just immigrated to Pittsburgh to join them."

"All those names ending in vowels! If only Mom could have seen this," Nick says. Dante nods in sad agreement.

Cecilia's three years with Barry in D.C. have changed their lives completely. Mostly, it was the twins—Andres and Ana—who did that. After Cecilia's first year there, it hadn't been marriage so much that Barry didn't want. It was a wedding. So they "eloped" to the Dominican Republic, where Barry's mom, grandmother, and two brothers' families attended the wedding in a small chapel. Barry's gracious mother Elin made Cecilia feel a welcomed part of their family. On birthday and Mothers' Day, Elin sends "To-my-daughter" greeting cards, rather than "daughter-in-law."

Cecilia is aware she's struggling with postpartum blues and with a renewed grief at her mother's absence. All new moms must look for help from their own mom. A mom who remembers giving birth and can rejoice over having grandchildren. But she's come to be grateful for her mother-in-law.

Elin has maintained the Bethesda, Maryland, condo that she and Barry's dad had owned. Cecilia and Barry were able to live there when they first came to D.C. They moved to a two-bedroom rental in D.C. two months before the twins were born.

Elin came for three weeks during the twins' second month. She slept on a cot in the room where the babies shared one crib. She brought her guitar, and her playing calmed them at night. Cecilia cried when Elin had to return home. But then Joan came every other weekend—the sisters had missed one another. Joan also slept in the twins' bedroom and did night duty.

The now-rested Cecilia began taking the twins to a neighborhood park. There she discovered that D.C. is full of moms pushing twins in strollers! Meeting other twin moms boosted her spirits—commiserating on the difficulties and sharing helpful advice. They're good friends now. *We're even talking about local schools. Most of our kids will be going to school together before long!*

Under the pandemic lockdown, the coronavirus has spread to meat-packing plants, prisons, and homeless shelters. Hospitals are overcome with cases. No one had envisioned anything this bad. Cecilia's cell rings—it's Joan—her lifeline to the outside world, or at least to Sarasota.

"Hey," Cecilia says.

"Did you hear that Cardinal Dolan's campaigning for Trump?" Joan asks. "He got hundreds of American bishops in on a phone call with the President—who assured them he's the most pro-Catholic president in America's history. Whatever that means!"

"It means anti-abortion," Cecilia says. "And that's America's head Cardinal urging Catholics to vote *against* the Catholic Joe Biden!" Her voice drops, "It's impossible to talk about the pandemic without getting into politics. And the pandemic's all everybody's talking about now."

"Has Dad relaxed his policy about not talking politics now?"

"Not that I know of, but I haven't talked to him in a while," Joan says. "Other news is that—after hardware stores—the next best-selling categories are home exercise equipment and clothing in larger sizes. Do those two seem a contradiction in terms? Dad and I both bought treadmills—hoping to avoid buying larger-size clothes."

"Good to hear, since most people are spending time at home cooking comfort food," Cecilia says.

"I'm doing the fasting diet and losing weight. It's cured me of the habit of late-night snacking." Joan says. "Dad's losing weight too."

"He's been hard to get ahold of. Dad doesn't usually answer his phone in the evenings when the stores are closed. If he does, he's always in a rush to get off, like maybe he's in the car." Cecilia says. "I wondered if he's out buying food at drive-throughs, but you're saying that's not it. So where is he?"

"Funny you should ask. We're gonna find out," Joan replies. "I just got the tracker APP on his cell phone. Last night he was at that Episcopal Church downtown. Perhaps working with that female priest? But in a closed church? Or out on benches in its yard? Why not online?"

"Is she attractive?" Cecilia asks.

"She's a forty-something woman who stays fit. Wicked smart," Joan says.

"Tall?" Cecilia asks.

"Average height—maybe five-eight-or so."

"Maybe they're looking at renderings—stuff too difficult to show on a phone. But keep checking; this could be interesting. Gotta run, Barry's done feeding both kids."

Later, Cecilia is changing Ana's diaper when her cell beeps, and she sees Joan's "CALL ME." *Something's happened*, Cecilia knows. She finishes diapering Ana, lifts her up, and walks into the kids' bedroom tapping Joan's number.

"It's Frank," Joan says. "He's got Covid."

"How on earth?" Cecilia asks. "He never goes out, does he?"

"His son Paul—the one in North Port—has a college kid named Jacob who was at the Florida beaches during spring break. None of those kids wore masks. So before that kid knew he had it, he exposed Frank. The kid got a light case, but Frank's sounds bad. He's eighty-five. An ambulance took him to the hospital this morning."

"No!" Cecilia cries. Barry rushes into the room carrying Andres, looking puzzled, then shocked at Cecilia in tears, yelling: "It should have been that fucking asshole kid! Is that shithead crazy? He gave Frank Covid!" Barry juggles Andres on one hip while lifting a now crying Ana away from Cecilia. Both babies are screaming as she rushes out of the room.

Emerging Life

At the end of March, playwright Terrance McNally is the first person in Sarasota to die of the new virus. By early April, nursing homes and hospitals are filled with Covid patients. Vaccines are reportedly in development, but no one knows when they might be available: only that whenever they come, the elderly will get them first.

Facing rapidly escalating coronavirus cases, Governor DeSantis issues a stay-at-home order on April 1. Florida businesses, beaches, and schools are closed; Easter and Passover services are virtual. DeSantis is condemned for the closures by a swarm of Libertarians claiming what was needed instead was "informed free choice and responsible free will." Cecilia sides with the governor on his cautious measures, not with her fellow Libertarians. *No one has a right to infect others.*

Dante and Abigail meet most evenings on the beautifully landscaped grounds behind her empty downtown church. Dante brings disinfectant wipes to the meetings for the arms of their benches and moves them six feet apart so they can sit, across from each other, masked, to discuss the project. And other things. Mostly other things lately.

Animals have taken over much of the church garden— even much of downtown—now. Ospreys screech while landing in the palm trees, some with large fish from the bay in their talons. Squirrels now claim their ground, no longer skittish around people. Geckoes scoot across the paving. A possum comes and goes.

Abigail's gray roots show now as her blonde hair has darkened. Dante finds that endearing. She's beautiful, masked, with gray hair and all. One evening, Abigail recalls his confession story, asking what he had doubted at age twelve.

"I'm not sure now, maybe papal infallibility. Back then, my mom had said her generation rejected the Vatican's verdict that the pill was sinful. She felt that never-married old men who run the Church were wrong about that. Mom wasn't giving us permission for sex, but if we went that route, she wanted her sons to be responsible. Mothers of sons worry their boys will get trapped by an irresponsible or conniving girl; parents of *daughters*—I've found—worry that the boys will take advantage of *them*!"

"I'm from an all-girl family, so I can support that last part!" Abigail laughs. "Did you see Trump saying he won't wear a mask? He thinks *it's not manly!* Wouldn't want to host heads of states—or the Queen!—wearing a mask."

"Yeah," Dante says. "Ignoring that, one: heads of state wouldn't visit during a pandemic. But two: if the Queen did come, it'd be a courtesy to greet her wearing a mask. She'd be wearing one."

Abigail holds up her arms to show him the back of her hands. "My skin's raw from all the hand washing. Whoever thought of singing Happy Birthday twice to time washing your hands?—that's crazy-making."

"Frank Bisignano says two Hail Marys, which is easier," Dante says, "depending on, I guess, if that prayer is meaningful to you."

"Some Episcopalians might call devotion to Mary a cult," she says, smiling.

"Are they the ones who've never heard Pavarotti sing *Ave Maria*?" he asks, laughing. "Some folks would say the whole 'eat-my-body-drink-my-blood' thing is a cult."

"Touche!" she says, smiling. "Did you find yourself praying to Mary more after your wife died?"

"Probably," he says. "But at that time my doubt about everything to do with religion was in full flower!"

"That all makes sense, especially when you'd been through such a great loss. How do you think you've emerged?"

"Back in college—in the prior millennium!—I used to discuss Pascal's Wager with a friend. They wager to live and try to believe as if God exists. If you're right, you have an infinite reward. But if you're wrong, you haven't really lost anything."

"Especially since you'll never know it!" Abigail says, smiling. Then adds: "And it would not have been a selfish life."

It's getting dark, and Dante starts wiping his bench with Clorox wipes. As she starts to gather her things, Abigail says, "In seminary, my Hebrew Bible teacher saw the Old Testament as the story of God searching for man. And a good Jew is one who searches for humility, contrition, and good deeds. I think he'd view you as a righteous Jew—constantly doing mitzvahs and enjoying your quest for them! If you weren't whatever kind of Catholic you are."

There's a smile beneath Dante's mask, as he continues to wipe the bench.

"No one else uses these benches," she tells Dante. "And they're outdoors. I don't think you need to worry about wiping them." She pauses, then asks, "Are you afraid of getting the virus—of not being there for your daughters?"

"No," he says, not turning around. Wiping the bench's arm, he says, "My fear isn't getting it. It's *giving* it."

"Why?" she asks. "Have you had symptoms?"

"No, no." He sits down suddenly on his bench, looking as if he wants to speak but can't.

"What's wrong, Dante?"

He sighs and drops his head, his hands holding used wipes dangling between his knees.

"It was me," he says.

"What was? I don't understand."

He looks directly at Abigail and says, "I was the one. Who phoned Lilliana. She was talking to me when she got hit by the car." He removes his glasses and pinches the bridge between his eyes. Abigail gasps. "Oh, no. I'm so sorry. But that was an accident." She stands and walks over to grab Dante's hand. "Dante, please stand up."

He stands.

"I need to hug you. For both of us. You won't make me sick. Permission to hug?"

Granted. He cooperates as she hugs him, burying her face under his chin. "I'm so, so sorry." She feels his deep shuddering.

Speaking softly, she asks, "Do your daughters know?"

"No, I don't ever want to burden them with that." He takes a deep breath. "I've never told another soul."

"We're going to be careful, Dante, for as long as it takes. Do everything possible. There's no blame. No fault. No matter what happens. Do you believe me?"

Silence, only Dante's shuddering.

"Do you believe me?"

"Yes." His voice is husky.

Still hugging him, Abigail adds. "It wasn't your fault with Lilliana. You weren't driving that car. It was terrible, hideous bad luck. And from now on when we part, I'm going to give you a backwards hug. OK?"

"Yes," he says quietly.

After a silence, with Abigail still hugging him, Dante's hoarse voice says: "Secrecy is so horrible," and her eyes fill with tears as she holds onto him.

A snowy egret's lacy feathers sway from behind its head and down its long neck, as it walks quietly a short distance in front of them, step-by-step on bright yellow feet, all the way to the street, which it crosses. Above, a large brown fox squirrel with a black face flies—like a glider plane—from a high oak tree branch to another tree, quite far away.

###

TO: CeciliaPR@gmail.com
FROM: JoanAceHW@srq.com
RE: Dad

He's with the female priest again tonight. St. Francis Project doesn't require evening meetings. Looks like Dad's dating during a pandemic!

TO: JoanAceHW@srq.com
FROM: CeciliaPR@gmail.com
RE: !!

What do you think of her?

TO: CeciliaPR@gmail.com
FROM: JoanAceHW@srq.com
REPLY: I like her

If Dad's serious about her, I'm good. You?

TO: JoanAceHW@srq.com
FROM: CeciliaPR@gmail.com
REPLY: Same

But why isn't he talking to us about this? Is he even talking to HER about it? Odd couple: Cafeteria & Episcopal priestess. What are the guidelines? During pandemic? Wonder if Uncle Nick knows anything?

TO: JoanAceHW@srq.com
FROM: CeciliaPR@gmail.com
REPLY: Ask Uncle Nick

Keep me informed.

###

With churches and synagogues suspending live services, Vera has lost her job during weekend masses, and school is now completely virtual. Since Malena's caregiving assignments are predominately in Sarasota, some distance away, and Vera is now home alone all the time, Joan invites her mother and daughter to move in with her.

Malena is in Joan's guest bedroom, and Vera sleeps on a daybed in Joan's Florida room, using a laptop for school that Joan no longer uses. Vera now has an adult with her much of the time when she isn't attending classes virtually. Once in a while, all three of them enjoy dinner and TV together.

Joan and Parker are together only by texting or a phone call; mostly talking about the pandemic. It's all anybody talks about now. "Have a nice day" has disappeared and the most common goodbye has been replaced with "Stay well" or "Be safe."

Sitting on benches in the church garden in early May, Dante tells Abigail, "Cecilia seems consumed with rage against this kid, Jacob, who exposed Frank to the virus. I don't know the kid, but I know how he must despair over causing his granddad to get Covid. I'm upset with him too, but I think of him going through life with this awful burden. I wish I could defuse Cecilia's anger. Her husband Barry confirms my worry that she's consumed with it."

His phone beeps, and Dante tells her, "It's Paul, Frank's son—Jacob's dad," before tapping it to say, "Hey, Paul. What's up?"

"Dad can't breathe. He's on a ventilator now. Doesn't look good."

"I'm so sorry for all the pain this is causing you and Jake," Dante says. "If there's anything I can do…" Dante knows there's nothing he can do.

"Thanks. I'll keep you informed," and they sign off.

Dante looks at Abigail. "Frank's on a ventilator. I don't want to tell the girls yet. It'll just make everything worse." Dante sits in a non-characteristic slump, looking down at his knees.

His head is bowed, sad.

Abigail says, "Cecilia's outraged because she thinks the kid should have known better. Those spring break photos of packed beaches upset us all. How old is Jacob?"

"He's a college freshman, so eighteen? nineteen?" Dante says. "He's dropped out of school now. Paul says he just hides in his room, playing video games."

"A neuroendocrinologist I studied under at Stanford wrote about the part of the brain that would've prevented a fully mature person from going to that beach—impulse control, postponing gratification. These functions are just not there until age twenty-five. That's why adolescents take such risks—their frontal cortex isn't fully developed. Might this article help Cecilia?" Abigail asks.

"I hope so. Yes, I'd like to send it to her. If there'd been an enforced stay-at-home order pertaining to beaches and bars during spring break, those kids wouldn't have been showing up in droves," Dante says. "Nursing homes were already filled with Covid. People dying. Now it's a hot mess." He pauses. "But Cecilia's anger at Jacob only complicates things."

"Yeah," Abigail says. "Cecilia needs to forgive Jacob. For her own good."

Dante walks Abigail to her car, then on the way to his car sees an animal—unleashed—walking down the center of Palm Avenue. Where did it come from? *Un oh. Not a dog. Coyote!*

Pulling his cell out of his pocket, he quickly taps onto Pandora's Death Metal channel—readied for coyotes who've been reported downtown at night. The cacophony makes the coyote turn and run through an alley between buildings. *They hate this sound. Gotta be ready for them if you're out at night now.*

After a recent Florida Wildlife Commission advisory that coyotes hate loud noise, the very name of the Death

Metal genre made Dante suspect that it might be the best coyote deterrent available. He Googled some bands to make his anti-coyote selection, which just proved itself stellar. Dante gets into his car and starts driving up Palm Avenue, thinking *who woulda thought I'd be fending off coyotes downtown with music?*

Driving up Palm Avenue, Dante is suddenly reminded of a long-ago online date's craze for a local Death Metal band then unknown to him. *As I suspected, I can't stand Death Metal music. Fortunately, neither can coyotes.*

###

In mid-May, Parker calls Joan to tell her he has accepted a job as an assistant basketball coach at Georgia State University. He'd been picking the brain of a former coach there all last season, asking advice on workouts and balancing his team. They'd texted and had a few very helpful phone chats. He had no idea it would lead to a job offer.

The pay is not much greater than he gets now as a high school coach, but his two sons from a long-ago divorce will have tuition-free college at Georgia State, as will Parker for work on his master's degree. Joan notes the tone of apology—*regret?*—in Parker's voice, as he relays this news. He has to be there in mid-June, for summer practice. She's unable to muster an enthusiastic tone as she congratulates him and wishes him luck. They both are aware of the loss of what had seemed promising and that he has no real choice but to take this opportunity for his boys and himself.

"I want to keep in touch and know what's in your life—and in Vera's," he says. He tells her he talked to Ursula Shaw, a school guidance counselor, about Vera's potential and her need for help with college applications, grants, scholarships—"everything necessary to assure she's led to the best package and choice. That process needs to start first thing, junior year."

Joan promises to be on top of it.

Covid has restricted their fully exploring a relationship, she knows. *But even if it hadn't, there's no way he could turn this down, and my work is in Sarasota.* She regrets having allowed herself to hope, now that she has to deal with the loss of what might have been. Hard enough to deal with everything else.

###

With Memorial Day approaching, Trump re-Tweets a fan's comment calling for Dr. Fauci, America's Chief Medical Advisor, to be fired for stating that a substance President Trump had touted to fight Covid is ineffective and can be dangerous. Online sites claim that Covid exists only as a Democratic plot to crash the stock market so that Trump won't be re-elected. People are beginning to rebel against wearing masks.

The Morettis are able to distance masked Ace customers six feet apart as they wait in line to pay, and employees will take purchases out to the car of any customer who won't wear a mask inside. By mid-June, eighty percent of Americans think the country is out of control—by the virus, by denials about it, and with arguments about masks. Public health officials face harassment, threats, and intimidation online and at their homes. Some resign due to death threats.

Right- and left-wing politicians claim the other side sparks the violence that's erupting.

America's enemies see a weak, divided, self-endangered United States.

16
Never Again Carefree/Third Quarter, August

Frank has died. His son Paul grieves that their family could not be with him in the end. His grandson Jacob is devastated. Dante informs the girls. He keeps the call to Cecilia brief. Her anguish is too much for him now, and he counts on Barry to help her.

Dante calls Paul, asking, "Can I come and see Jake?"

"He's not talking, but you're welcome to come."

"I don't know that I can be of any help, but I'll be checking on stores in Osprey and Venice and Port Charlotte—so will be in your neighborhood, so to speak. I can stop by late midday if that suits you."

"You're welcome here at any time," Paul says.

While Dante doesn't really need to visit his stores south of Sarasota, he decides he might as well make a day of doing so while in that area for what he feels compelled to do: talk to Jacob. It's an overcast day as he crosses the junction entering Myakka River State Park, and across the cloudy sky he notices a couple of black birds. *Uh oh, vultures. Something's dead. Raccoon? Armadillo? Four circling up there now. The dead thing's big if that many vultures.*

Distracted for seconds, he suddenly sees a large circular mass on the road—*what?*—in his path. Swerving toward the shoulder of the highway to miss it, Dante then sees that the increasing mass of vultures are circling a dead wild boar, highly bloated. It lies just beyond the shoulder of the road.

Back on the highway and somewhat shaken, Dante realizes that the boar had been decapitated by whatever hit it. *Had to be a semi—that thing's bigger than me. Those boars run a hundred-fifty pounds or more, and it's so bloated it's been there for a couple of days. Looks ready to explode.* He's relieved that he avoided running over the boar's head. Its tusks would have blown a tire.

Drivers are speeding at night these days of little traffic, and wild boars tend to start roaming at dusk. Huge problem. He knows that several counties around the tiny houses average two wild boars an acre. They'll attack humans, and their tusks are deadly.

Dante feels even more relieved after visiting the Osprey and Venice stores; business is good and managers are handling the safety measures. He needed those visits to cool down after that close call on the highway.

In North Port, Dante pulls into the Bisignano driveway and is greeted by Paul, who is outside, blowing leaves.

Obviously happy to see Dante, Paul takes him inside and offers coffee.

"No, thanks. I'm good," Dante replies, ready to get down to the business of seeing Jacob. They walk down a hallway, and Paul raps on Jake's door, opens it, and says "Dante's here to say hello." Paul shuts the bedroom door, as Dante's saying, "I'm so sorry for your loss, Jake. I came to tell you about something that happened to me…"

###

Minutes later, Dante's sitting at the end of the bed, talking to Jake, who sits in a chair facing his computer screen. "In all this time, I've told only one other person, who's helped me see that—as in your case—it was dumb bad luck. I wasn't driving the car, though I unintentionally prevented my wife from seeing it. And it was bad luck that you unintentionally passed that virus to Frank. It was COVID that killed him, not you."

"I've never told my daughters this as it would only cause them more anguish. I'm telling you in confidence."

"Why?" Jake asks bluntly, staring at his computer screen through too much greasy hair. Dante gets a whiff of the kid's bad breath, even though they're not facing one another, realizing that he's not brushing his teeth, not bathing.

"Because, bad luck or not, I know the tremendous weight you carry," Dante says. "I came to tell you that you won't always feel crushed by it, as you do now. You won't have the carefree college years you deserve to have. But I also know you'll emerge from this with an acute feeling for others who grieve all kinds of bad luck or unfortunate choices. Someone else will need that from you someday. And that part of this—oddly enough and hard for you to believe now—will become a blessing. You can be happy again, Jake."

"I don't see happiness in my future." The boy's voice chokes as he speaks, still staring at his computer screen.

"I know," Dante says. "That leads to another reason I came—to offer you a job at Ace. Since you're not studying now—and I think that's a good decision—working this job may help you. Maybe distract you from your grief for a while."

"What would you want me to do at Ace?"

"It would be at our warehouse that serves all the stores. You'd be unloading merchandise, setting packages up for distribution to the different locations. Very little intermingling with people. You wouldn't have to put on a happy face. It would help us a great deal."

"When?"

"We need this help some days more than others. So, we could start slowly when bigger shipments arrive. It could lead to a full-time job eventually. I suggest we start two days a week, nine to five. Does that sound OK to you?"

"Can I think about it?"

"Of course. Give me your mobile number and I'll text you my contact info. If you'd let me know within a week, it would help. We need to fill the position." While handing Dante his phone, Jacob looks up to make eye contact for the first time.

"OK," Jacob says, his voice neutral. At Jacob's toneless reply, Dante thinks, *OK. He's neither for nor against. The door is open.*

###

After a brief but encouraging visit to the Ace store in Port Charlotte, Dante feels hopeful about Jacob. The day's been tiring, and now he wants to get past the site of the dead animal before dusk to assure he doesn't ride over those boar tusks. Sharp hunger makes him realize that he hasn't eaten all day. He needs to get a sandwich to go, take it home, and crash after this long day.

Concerned about his tires, he approaches Myakka Park, scanning the road to see if the smashed boar's head is still there. But his attention instead is suddenly drawn to the shoulder of the road where dozens of buzzards are swarming above—and some are on—the body. The rib cage and ribs are now visible. *They've pretty much picked that sucker clean. The efficacy of nature. Disgusting. But efficient.*

On the other side of the wild boar, Dante's relieved to find a good parking place at Publix. He rushes in, heading directly to the deli.

Drawing his number at the counter, he walks over to quickly grab a pre-packaged fruit across from the deli line and is soon back seeing his number posted. Looking at the meats Dante can't rid his mind of images of the buzzards feasting on the carcass. He flinches as he hands his ticket to a gray-haired man who's wiping his hands on his once-white apron.

"What'll it be, sir?" the guy asks.

"Sandwich, please, on a whole wheat bun, couple slices of cheddar, mustard, pickle, ham, and rare roast beef."

The deli man grabs the bun—slicing it open, he looks up at Dante through smudged glasses and asks, "D'ya want the Boar's Head?"

"NO!" Dante says, repulsed, startling the butcher. Then Dante remembers what the guy means: the name brand. "Publix brand deli meat's fine, thank you."

The Bishop Calls / September

Driving back from the development site, Abigail's surprised to see a text message from the church office asking her to return a call from Bishop Haskell Billings. Head of the Episcopal Diocese of Southeast Florida—the other coast. *What could he want to talk to me about?* They didn't connect until that evening. The bishop opens with: "The Diocese here wants you to explore moving to Miami to help bring your tiny house movement to the East Coast."

Abigail is stunned.

"We have seventy-six congregations in the diocese, and my Executive Director for Charities has identified five of the most likely candidates for the initial launch. We'd like your opinion on which one of the five to start with. And there are other matters to discuss, of course."

"I don't know what to say," Abigail replies. "I'm immersed in doing it in just one parish here. It involves work with so many entities—Veterans—the Amish—"

"We're enthusiastic about that inter-faith alliance—with the peace-loving Amish. It's one of many elements that appeal. We'd need your guidance, of course, since you've built a relationship with certain individuals. I understand that the Amish in several parts of the country make tiny houses of various kinds, offering possibilities of eventual expansion."

"It also requires funding," Abigail says. "I've built a unique relationship with the local Ace Hardware here."

"Our diocese will fund the first small community of homes," Bishop Billings says. "We don't anticipate future funding to be a problem. We'd expand to other congregations—with fundraising among the communities involved, and possible support from local businesses and congregations."

"You're envisioning a progression of building tiny house communities throughout Southeast Florida?" she asks, awed.

"Yes. I will send a car to Sarasota to bring you here— and back. I'm at the age to have had my first shot, but my staff is fully masked, and we will meet outdoors. Please come to discuss possibilities with our resource people—let them question you.

"I'm asking you to discern with us about what you've started, and where it might go. I understand you have a major commitment where you are. I honor that. I believe you'll want to seriously consider what I'm asking. I hope you'll leave us with a timeline of when you'll be able to move here to direct us with your God-given talents for helping our most unfortunate neighbors."

"We need you here on the East Coast," he says, firmly.

Abigail tells the bishop she'll come next month and will give him the date for her visit soon.

Housing street people throughout Florida—*that's a dream I didn't even have—coming true!* In bed that night, she's unable to sleep, aware that she's been developing a pattern to share with others who have the motivation and resources to do it elsewhere. Staring at the ceiling fan, she's come to realize *my only stumbling block is leaving Dante.* Sadly, it would be a major complication if there were any indication something personal might develop beyond their tiny home partnership. *Beyond our close what-ever-it-is-relationship, our shared interests, and—even—beliefs. Cafeteria Catholic that he claims to be. Whatever that means.*

She's always realized that *I'm the one who initiated hugs. My spontaneous way to reach out to him in his grief. It's come to mean more to me than consoling—ministering to—a dear friend. But where did I think this was going* anyway? *The Roman church is ingrained in Italian Dante.*

She turns, looking out the window at the slice of moon in the dark sky, and decides to set a date to visit Miami as soon as possible. *And pray that I make the choice most consistent with my possibilities, and expectations.*

She punches the pillow and puts her head on it, deciding she won't leave Sarasota until St. Francis Gardens is fully occupied.

The Last, Best Hope / September

At his workstation in a corner of the bedroom, Barry signs off for the day. It's been a good one. He knows he's fortunate to have found Bloomberg Philanthropies his ideal job. It's the former mayor's global effort to improve lives in areas where mayors make campaign promises—but once elected, can seldom think creatively: art and education, job creation, public health, and safety. Barry works in the climate change initiative, from home now, which is proving to be challenging in a house crowded with kids' stuff and stressed by storm warnings of Cecilia's constant anger.

The baseball card Dante sent is propped above his computer: Dr. Fauci throwing out the first ball at the opening of the season in D.C., wearing a Nat's uniform. After Fauci's pitch, players from both teams surrounded him to get his autograph on a ball. *Like a rock star*, Barry thinks, smiling. *No TOPPS card has ever sold or increased in value as quickly as this one.*

Dante treats me like the son he never had. Cecilia and Mom have the same bond. It's almost like when we married we both fulfilled a longtime need for the parents we lost. Though we didn't see it that way then.

It's dinner time, so he walks down the hall and then pulls aside a baby jumper hanging at the entrance to the dining area so he can enter the room and get Ana ready. Cecilia's anger exhausts her. And him. *I need patience. Is postpartum depression contagious?*

At the kitchen counter, Cecilia's focused on the kids' and adults' food. Barry goes over to pick up Ana, who sits on the kids' giant alphabet rug. The toy box is open, and she's got stuffed animals and dolls all over the floor.

He picks her up and puts her in the highchair across from the one Andres is already in. He and Cecilia alternate the baby each one tends every day so that Ana and Andres get equal private time with both parents. Barry is cutting Ana's hot dog into pieces now as Cecilia puts Andres's bib on.

He's arranged this whole day around this evening's treat. Baseball! Miami vs. Tampa. In empty stadiums. Barry thinks about tonight's teams. COVID hit Miami hard this season—twenty Marlins positive. In July, the Miami manager had never even met most of the new players on his bench. Now they're rockin'! Tampa looks even better. *BASEBALL. What this country needs right now. What I need now—if only Cecilia will do something else. In another room.*

"Dad seems to be dating Abigail during the pandemic." Cecilia's tone is neutral.

"Are you OK with it?" Barry asks.

"Yeah. He needs a good woman in his life." Cecilia sighs, then adds, "I wish he hadn't enlisted her to help me deal with Frank's death."

"I found the article they sent helpful. Did you?" he asks. *Alacantara pitching for Miami tonight—All-Star—and they just acquired the best hitter on the market, Marte. Both Dominicans.*

"I get the point, that I shouldn't hold Jacob responsible because of his immaturity. But deep down I believe that when I was his age," she says, "I'd have listened to the science, appreciated the risk. If I had gone to the beach and bar, I'm pretty sure I wouldn't have spent time with my grandparents right after that."

"Yeah," Barry says, helping Ana with a bite. "You were probably more mature at that age than Jake is. Girls usually are. But mostly I think you'd have been cautious because those of us who lost a parent very young are programmed to be more fearful about the parents and grandparents we still have. More protective of them." Microwave clock says 6:45 pm.

"Frank was my consolation after losing Nani," Cecilia says. "He encouraged me to come to D.C., to make that big decision to leave my family. I'm aware of what I'd have missed—and regretted—if I hadn't come." She smiles, weakly, at Barry.

"I suspect that your dad and Abigail know more than they shared when they sent you the article. Jacob's dropped out of school, which sounds like depression. I wonder if he's suicidal," Barry says.

"Omigod. Don't lay that on me too," she says.

"I'm not making you responsible for Jacob. Just trying to imagine all this grief—in a pandemic," Barry says. "Abigail's a minister. I'm guessing she and Dad hope you'll be able to forgive the kid, for your own sake. Worried that anger's dragging you down." *Dragging both of us down! They're singing the "Star Spangled Banner."*

Ana is done, so Barry wipes her hands and face and lifts her out of the highchair and carries her toward the TV. "Ana and I are gonna watch TV for a while." Barry's raised eyebrows suggest an 'OK?' He moves toward Cecilia for a kiss. She deflects it, and he thinks, *We both need to stay apart for now.*

He winds his way through the room, which is strewn with superhero capes and princess skirts, cars and trucks, and a miniature kitchen. Stepping over to the Chicco talking farm, he remembers that it's bi-lingual, all two-hundred-fifty words of it. With songs and flashing lights. It overstimulates both parents, who vow not to acquire any more toys with sounds. Or batteries.

Which has proven impossible.

Barry hopes that Cecilia will take Andres to bed, so the living room can be his. Although evidence reveals that it actually belongs to the kids. He puts Ana in a baby jumper with its own stand and toy tray and picks up the remote. Plopping down on the couch, he remains tense, yet hopeful. He clicks on the game: *Baseball—my last, best hope to get through 2020.*

Dante's Resolve

It's been a good day. Dante's scale shows a forty-pound total loss. The 2020 goal was met! This evening he takes a Frontera Chicken Verde Dinner Bowl out of the freezer and reads the nutrition label:

Calories 270

Total Fat 4.5 g

He pops the plastic cover with a fork and puts it in the microwave. Watching the bowling circle, Dante thinks: *Feeling good. Tonight I'm going to talk to Abigail about us. Ask some questions. About her intentions. Declare mine? We'll see. Start the conversation. I'm ready.*

As he eats, the TV reports that many colleges have suspended students or fraternities for gathering in large groups to party, ignoring protective guidelines. Governor DeSantis is shown saying that suspending these outlaw students is "incredibly draconian." He's drawing up a "bill of rights" for college kids to party.

"That's what college kids do," the governor says.

"Not in a pandemic," Dante groans to the on-screen DeSantis, thinking, *with Florida's highest death toll yet and 200,000 Americans dead. In a pandemic, none of us does what we usually do. We're all in this together.* Dante's sadness over what unmasked college partying did to Frank—and to Jacob—floods him once more. He flicks off the TV and goes into the bedroom to change clothes.

He gets out the J. Peterman clothes Joan gave him for Father's Day and pulls on what J. P. calls the Officer and a Gentleman pants. "Think of them as Dress Khakis," Peterman advises in his catalog, then adds—as only Peterman can—"You may not be an officer. But you can't stop being a gentleman."

These clothes were also meant to celebrate Dante's weight loss. He's nervous when pulling the top (the Russian Navy Shirt) over his head. It's a blue-and-white striped long-sleeved knit. Horizontal stripes! Looking in the mirror, he thinks *better than expected.* But his lifelong aversion to horizontal stripes makes him glad this evening is cool enough for Peterman's Irish Mariner's Cardigan. The final piece in Joan's package is a kind of shirt jacket the catalog claims is "in a double-breasted seafaring style, painstakingly woven from buttery-soft but dense cotton." *Where do they find people to write this stuff?* But looking in the mirror, Dante feels good.

Abigail. See Abigail tonight. Get away from today's dismal news. On to Something hopeful.

Don't fuck it up.

Mating for Life

Sitting on her bench as Dante arrives, Abigail puts an index finger up to her masked lips, a "shhhh" gesture. With her other hand, she points left. As he steps quietly into the garden looking left, he sees two sandhill cranes. He freezes. Each bird is at least four feet tall, with multi-gray feathers from white to almost black. Their bright red heads make him think: *like a Catholic Cardinal's skull cap, their zucchetto.* Dante remains still, as they walk toward the curb. Each bird steps elegantly into the street and keeps walking.

"I think they're a threatened species," he says quietly as he sits down on the bench facing her.

"They are. And they mate for life," Abigail replies quietly, like Dante, not wanting to scare the birds.

"Funny you should bring that up," Dante says, laughing at this unexpected opportunity to get to his point so quickly. "I've been wondering if you'd been seeing anyone else…perhaps dating someone from your parish?"

"No. I'm not. I have a policy of not dating members of my congregation."

"Why?"

"Well, think of, one—the gossip. No one is able to resist passing that news along! Then two—what happens if or when you break up? You're still on parish committees and in activities together. So three—*that* gossip!"

"Right," Dante says, emboldened. "I never thought of any of that. I just thought of all those attractive Episcopalian men, looking like George Bush in his younger days. Either George Bush younger. Weren't most of our Presidents Episcopalian?" *With JFK a minority of one!* he thinks. "I believe so," she says, "but who's counting?" They both laugh. "Other than us!"

After Dante became involved in the tiny house project, he went to Abigail's church. He knew the Mass would be similar to that day's Catholic Mass, even with the same Bible readings. What was different was the people. Episcopalians come well dressed—no teenagers walking up to communion in shorts and tee shirts with obnoxious slogans, like at Catholic Mass. *Some older women reminded me of Barbara Bush, stately/matronly; younger ones mostly anchor-woman-attractive. No obesity—that's lower-income folks. Very few people of color, unlike St. Martha's—or any Catholic Church I've ever been to.*

"Any more questions for me?" Abigail asks.

"Well, yes. Have we been…dating?"

They laugh again. "Well, I don't know if it can be called dating in a pandemic," Abigail says, "but I know my Canadian grandmother would say we've been 'keeping company'."

"Meaning, with an honorable intention to…?" Dante waits to see if she will finish.

"Yes, it generally means the two are thinking of a long-term commitment."

"Marriage!" Dante, exultant that he'd said it.

"Yes, assuming that's mutually agreeable." Her blue eyes above her mask reveal that she's smiling.

"I'm the happiest man in the world right now," Dante exhales a long sigh. "May I make a confession?"

"Of course," she says. "You're very good at confessions."

"I love you, Abigail Curtis."

"I love you too, Dante Moretti."

Father Mario's Challenge

Cecilia and Barry are joining the Moretti and Bisignano family members online, to celebrate a virtual Mass in memory of Frank. "Celebrate" is what this white-haired pastor Mario Salotto does, Cecilia thinks, recalling the joy he put into the Mass for Nani a few years ago.

The screen shows Father Mario at the altar in an empty St. Martha's Church. Another priest stands far behind him at a lectern. Father Mario removes his mask to smile and say, "Welcome, my friends. Let us celebrate this Mass…"

Passages from Isaiah and the Psalms read by the other priest seem to speak to this time of turmoil. After the reading from Matthew's Gospel, Father Mario asks: "Have you loved? Have you taken care of the poor? Do you bring peace? Or are you the children of fighting, of force, of greed? Let's show that we are the people of light, of love, the people who try to be united as peacemakers. Let's offer prayers for our messy world today." His Italian accent seems to add gravity to his questions.

They recite the *Prayers of the Faithful:*

"For police, health-care providers, firefighters, keep them healthy and safe;

"For the president, governors, senators, that all civil servants unite to lead us in peace in these uncertain times;

"For all who died from Coronavirus, especially Frank Bisignano, may he rest in peace."

Asking for the Lord's Prayer, Father Mario looks straight at his viewers to say, "It's time to forgive: Pray now for the one who broke your heart."

Cecilia bursts into tears, thinking *Pray for Jacob when I'm so angry at him!* That night, in bed, staring up in the dark, Cecilia whispers an Our Father "for Jacob Bisignano," tears running down her face.

###

TO: CeciliaPR@gmail.com
FROM: JoanAceHW@srq.com
Re: Yes, Dad's dating her.

He's lost weight, quit smoking, & works out—the healthiest we've ever known him. Have to be happy for him—while I'm also thinking: shouldn't that be me—or me too!

TO: JoanAceHW@srq.com
FROM: CeciliaPR@gmail.com
RE: Wedding in her church?

Can anyone plan a wedding in the pandemic?

TO: CeciliaPR@gmail.com
FROM:JoanAceHW@srq.com
RE: Dad & Abigail

She's divorced. No kids. With married priests, you gotta figure half of those priests will end up divorced—statistically speaking. Like everyone else. Can't see it in a crowded church with people we don't know! But I hope to look better whenever that time comes. No reason to dress up/wear makeup now. Hideous hair.

TO: JoanAceHW@srq.com
FROM: CeciliaPR@gmail.com
Re: Hair

Salons closed here too. I'm going for a Rapunzel look. What do you pay for a haircut in DC? I have to keep working just to cover salon visits. One appt in DC is often $250—with highlights/cut/toner/tip. Spending up to $500/month pre-pandemic. Your gorgeous red hair saves you a fortune!

TO: CeciliaPR@gmail.com
FROM: JoanAceHW@srq.ccom
RE? DC salon vs. Sarasota

Cut here $50. It's the highlights etc. breaking your bank. Does Barry know your salon $$$?

TO: JoanAceHW@srq.com
FROM: CeciliaPR@gmail.com
REPLY: NO!

Why are men's haircuts so much cheaper at the same salon? Total Sexual discrimination. Gotta get RBG on that.

Texting from their beds at night, both sign off and turn off their lights. The next morning Cecilia gets the news online, then texts her sister: "RBG's death just announced in DC."

TO: CeciliaPR@gmail.com
FROM: JoanAceHW@srq.com
RE: RIP RBG

There'll never be another RBG. Kween of the Kourt.

17

Poetry in Motion Fourth Quarter, October

Cecilia has glimmers of feeling like her old self again, after a long time of darkness. She's surprised to find that praying for Jacob seems to be helping her. She hears that Jacob's attending a Zoom support group led by a therapist. They're all kids who went out to party and then infected a loved one who died. Now trying to deal with their own grief and shame. Maybe Dad giving Jacob a job will help him. Maybe prayers are helping him too. *Maybe they're helping me forgive him.*

Gratitude helps. Cecilia is thankful now: *for Frank when I needed him. For the twins. For my Sarasota family. Mostly for Barry. My everything. Finally, someone under my roof who discusses politics with me.* Evolving from a party-focus to goal-focused political opinions we can work with and live with.

She recalls Uncle Nick telling her that his Cuban wife Liberty has never voted for a Democrat in her life, her parents having escaped Castro's Communism. Ancestors of one of the twin moms—Carmen—in the park fled Francisco

Franco, so Carmen votes against right-wing Republicans. Both parties accuse each other of extremist positions. Centrists seem to have disappeared.

Cecilia's news site reports that the President and Mrs. Trump, three Senators, and four White House aides are confirmed positive for Covid. The prior day, the President—unmasked and having tested positive—appeared at a New Jersey fundraiser with over two hundred unmasked attendees. *Trump's gone from being the mask-denier to a super spreader*, Cecilia thinks, frightened, shutting off CNN on her cell and pocketing it. She's aware that Barry's suffered from her dark time.

How long since we last had sex? Too long. I'll make it up to him.

Amid everything else, tonight is Game One of the MLB postseason. Tampa Rays vs. Yankees. As the first pitch is thrown, an eager Barry thinks—objectively, he believes—that the Rays are the better team, with Snell, the Rays most consistent starting pitcher, so if he'll be rested if they have to go to a Game five. The Yankees are home run hitters, but Snell dominated Toronto in the Wild Card round—which had several home run hitters too.

At 9:00 p.m., sitting on their two-cushion loveseat in front of the TV, Barry leans down to Andres on his lap, whispering, "If only Momma goes to bed so we can watch the game." Barry didn't clean up the kitchen as he often does, leaving that to occupy Cecilia if she should enter the room after getting Ana to bed. She'll probably get into bed herself, though, he hopes. Barry leans down to clap the baby's hands together, quietly saying, "We gotta root-root-root for our BayRays, OK?" Andres gurgles a happy consent.

So far, so good: into the fifth inning. A Yankee home run evens the score at 3–3. Snell can't seem to locate his fastball. Watching the Yankees score to break into the lead, Barry doesn't see Cecilia enter the room.

"How's it going?" she asks.

Barry says, "Not so good for Tampa right now," dismayed at hearing her voice.

Cecilia plops down next to him on their small loveseat, asking, "Can I join you two?" Not waiting for an answer, she says, "I'm outraged at these debates about masking. Both sides talking about freedom. Libertarians leaning toward Trump's so-called freedom NOT to wear a mask." She continues talking to Barry's profile, as he watches TV. "It's giving in to fear and rage. You can be shamed or attacked…at Safeway!"

Barry keeps his eyes fixed on the game, willing Cecilia: *Go to bed. Go AWAY. This isn't pandemic time—it's BASEBALL time. My time!*

"How do lockdowns and masking thwart liberty if the outcome is a deadly disease?" she asks. An exasperated Barry turns to her, trying to say calmly, "Cec, it isn't that I prefer watching baseball to an evening with you, but the game's at a crucial point now." He prefers watching baseball.

She gets up and goes to the fridge, holds up a beer, cocks her head as if to ask, "Want one?" Barry shakes his head no.

Returning to the loveseat with her Never Say Never craft brew, she says, "Masks are a small price to pay in a pandemic. Frank didn't find freedom in the hospital, or the cemetery."

The eighth inning is over, and as the teams change, Barry says, "Honey, I gotta pee. Will you put Andres to bed?" He hands a sleeping Andres over, gets up, and moves quickly. He doesn't need to pee; he needs a break from Cecilia's chatter. He waits some time then flushes, hoping that after she puts Andres' nighttime diaper on and gets him down, she'll not return to the living room.

He creeps back to the couch as the ninth inning starts. Then hears Cecilia's voice, coming back in.

"—Anti-maskers carry 'Brave & Free' signs. Like I have no right to safety from their virus droplets when they yell at me."

Ninth inning: Yankees at bat. Two on base. *We gotta get outta this. One more out. C'mon.*

Shit! Another on; bases loaded with Yankees. The Rays got out of loaded bases earlier, but…"For years, the Tea Party influenced the GOP to defund NIH, CDC—through Ebola and predictions of the pandemic." Cecilia's rant continues. "Trump's proposed more cuts to—"

Grand slam! "Fuck!" Barry jumps up and turns to holler at Cecilia. "Will you stop? I couldn't have a moment's peace to watch this game. If you'd only let me watch, this wouldn't have happened."

Babies start crying. "See what you've done *now*?" Barry yells, pointing to the bedroom.

"Wait: I woke them up?" Cecilia jumps up. Walking to the twins' bedroom, she stops at the door to the hallway to turn and shout at Barry, "And you hold me responsible for that last inning? It's *my* fault the Rays lost? Seriously?"

"Everything's your fault!" Barry yells. "Your doom and gloom about the way the pandemic's handled by politicians who're trying to figure out this awful mess. They're afraid of *both* Covid and businesses closing, people losing their jobs, unable to pay their rent or feed their kids. They don't know what to do because we've never been here before, and it just keeps getting worse no matter what they do. Or where. Or who's doing it."

He grabs his coat and keys, and stops to shout: "How do we ever know we're a force for good? How do you? We all just muddle along, going by our own experience, our prejudices, our fears—our ineptness!"

He slams the door as he leaves the house.

Cecilia enters the bedroom, puts the twins in her baby sling, and walks them. "It's OK kiddies. Daddy's had a breakdown," she tells them. "He's lost his mind. Everyone in this pandemic is going crazy—from the President on down to Daddy—who blames *me* for Tampa's loss!"

Cecilia pretended to be asleep when Barry came to bed last night. *He was upset last night with my anger. Tired of it. I'm tired of it too.* She got up, fed the kids, and is coming back with them from the park, aware that Barry waited for her to take them out as she does every morning, to avoid her.

Because he feels he was foolish to blame me for the loss? Or because he's still mad? As she wheels the twin stroller through the front door, he's at the kitchen table drinking coffee.

"Hey," she says as they approach him.

"Hi," he replies. She gives him Ana, takes Andres out, and sits across the table.

"Did you tell the moms in the park that I blamed you for the Rays' loss?" he asks, a sheepish grin on his face.

"Yeah," she says, smiling.

"So they think I'm an asshole?"

"They think you're hilarious." Both are smiling.

"OK, it was crazy. I was feeling you distracted me throughout the game, making me lose the mojo I was bringing the Rays. I know that sounds nutty, but—"

"No," Cecilia says. "Actually, I get it. That's why I'm going to watch the game with you tonight and be quiet. Winning mojo from both of us. Tonight the Rays will win. And I will not talk." Her right hand held up in a pledge. "I promise."

"OK. So from now on, the only place we cannot talk politics or the pandemic is during baseball games. OK?"

"Agreed." The moms know everyone's going crazy now. Covid surging to an all-time high after so long. We've been cooped up longer than we dreamt possible. Connie said, "We vowed 'for better or for worse', but not for eight months of twenty-four-seven togetherness." Cecilia gets up to put Andres in the highchair and brings the coffee pot to the table with a mug for herself.

"Baseball makes me remember my dad," Barry says. "You know how you lose so much memory of that parent who died. Just keeping the tiniest bits of things they said? Once when we were watching baseball, a Red Sox fielder—

Manny Ramirez—made an unbelievable catch. Ran like crazy all the while doing a full stretch, collapsing to the ground to get the ball just a second before it hit the grass.

"Watching that play, Dad said, 'That, my son, is poetry in motion.' I think of it when I see the physical beauty of the game now. Some plays are as beautiful as ballet. I want our kids to enjoy baseball."

"Yes! How true that we retain just a few odd statements our missing parent once said. The oddest ones stick in my mind," Cecilia says. "My memory is Mom once telling me, 'Purple is a neutral color. It goes with everything.'" She holds up her bag, "So I carry a purple purse!"

Barry gets up to lean down and kiss Cecilia. "I'm sorry."

"I'm sorry too. I was wound up with my own nonsense and blind to everything you wanted to concentrate on. Tonight, I promise, not a peep." She motions locking her lips.

As Cecilia promised, the Rays won Game Two. And Game Three. Double mojo victories. The Yankees won Game Four, so Game Five has to decide it. Barry and Cecilia will remember the end of Game Five for the rest of their lives. Tampa shortstop Brosseau faced Yankee pitcher Chatman, who'd recently thrown a 101-mph fastball at Brosseau's head. This time, Brosseau hit a bases-loaded home run, winning the Division victory. Justice!

As the Rays celebrate, Barry flicks his finger up his cell screen, reporting to Cecilia: "Brosseau didn't get picked for any MLB team out of college. The shortest guy on the team…among the bottom in salary on the Rays' skimpy payroll. That Yankee pitcher signed a three-year contract for $48 million. Brousseau signed for $563,500. Sweet!"

Barry's elated. It seems this exhilarating baseball postseason cured Cecilia of her depression! Painted her nails those light and dark blue Rays colors—fingers and toes! Got interested, involved, and learned players' names. *We'll enjoy every baseball season together now.*

He thinks back to his Little League days, smiling: teammates talking about their fate with girls in baseball terms. "Didn't even get to first base." Getting to second or third meant whatever imagination implied. No one got a home run at that age. Probably no one actually ever got beyond first. *Locker room bragging before we had locker rooms.*

He's confident now that he and Cecilia will celebrate this Division victory—after not being "beyond first base" for months. Baseball—of all things—has restored Cecilia. It's magic! He can tell she's newly charged—emotionally, and maybe sexually.

Barry was right. That night was a bases-loaded home run. Poetry in motion.

In the next round of playoffs, Barry and Cecilia enjoy "beatin' the cheatin' Astros," whose 2019 World Series title carries an asterisk to indicate cheating. The Rays lost the World Series to the Dodgers, but what a great season! Barry and Cecilia find hope. Vaccines are being approved. Thanksgiving is coming, and there's much to be thankful for at the end of the most stressful year of their lives.

Lockdown has forced a new way of living and of thinking about what's important: questioning safety advice against the need to open businesses, even—especially—how to get valid information. Self-sufficiency was overrated. All the Morettis feel that voting this year is more important than it's ever been in their lifetime. Yet even going to the polls might endanger their health.

Still, being alive and not afflicted offers a new cause for Thanksgiving as the holiday approaches—for workers on the front lines in hospitals and essential workers who pick up the garbage and keep groceries stocked. With Ana and Andres on their laps, Cecilia and Barry meet online with Dante, Joan, Paul, and Jacob, all thankful for Zoom and for one another. As rage and comeuppance rule Washington, and doom-scrolling and false social media rule the Internet, the Morettis in their Florida stores see civility and cooperation to get things done.

Some of their customers are still at work sites; others are remodeling and fixing their own homes while confined to them. And many of them are helping not-so-fortunate neighbors. Then, a winter wave of the virus pushes America's deaths to 200,000 a day and shows no signs of stopping. One American is dying of Covid every thirty-four seconds. The vaccine roll-out is slower than hoped. December becomes the worst month of the pandemic that has been raging for nine months.

Ace stores continue record business results, and by now the St. Francis Gardens Community has grown to house sixteen Veterans, with expansion underway in Miami.

18

Free at Last/2021

Early in February, while mowing his yard, Dante sees something so unusual on a tree limb that he has to look again when he comes back on his mower. Yes, a robin! They rarely migrate this far south. Must be the unusually frigid weather most everywhere else. Even Texas is snow- and ice-bound. In Laconia, they always welcomed robins as a sign of spring. *Here, it's a sign of frigid weather everywhere else. They'll be thirsty. Bring a bird bath home from the store tonight.*

By mid-June, the Covid death toll has topped the whole of 2020. There's a sharp divide between developed and developing countries. Vaccines have been available throughout America for certain demographics, and most cities have opened up. But variants are spreading now. There's still much to learn about this disease, and people suspect that life may never again be as it was before Covid.

Worse, even the vaccination has become politicized. Americans eager to get the shots and those who refuse them leave slightly less than half of the population vaccinated. Some businesses still require masks; others don't. All aware that their customers are divided on wearing one.

By August, Florida becomes the Covid epicenter of the nation, with the highest one-day total since the start of the pandemic. Hospitals are again overwhelmed; deaths are now among much younger victims—many of whom have been vaccine resisters.

In the midst of this, Dante wants to go to Mazzaro's Italian Market in St. Pete to shop for wine and freshly made pasta for their small outdoor wedding reception. They still wear masks when shopping among strangers in stores, knowing that widespread masking is what's necessary to stop transmission. Everyone is more in danger of Covid when masking is hit or miss, including the few who now wear masks.

Abigail has never visited this huge indoor farmer's market full of products for feasting, and Dante asks her to help select everything from hors d'oeuvres to tiramisu. With shopping bags placed in his cooler for the drive home, they approach a church when he says, "That's where I made that confession so long ago—with the good deed penance."

"Lots of cars," Abigail says. "Looks like a Saturday Mass going on."

"I wonder if Father Bede's still there," he says, suddenly turning into the drive. "If he is, I'd love to say hello and tell him that his long-ago Confession led me to you. OK with you to go in and see?"

"Let's do it. I'm curious to meet him," she says. Dante parks, and they enter the church, slipping into a pew in a back row. Seeing the familiar priest at the altar, Dante nudges Abigail, nodding to indicate he's Father Bede.

Mass is ending, but couples are walking toward the altar instead of the exit doors, and everyone else is staying in their pews. The couples stand facing their priest, who is now saying "… to have and to hold," the elderly group repeating it. *A wedding vow renewal!* Dante realizes.

After "until death do us part," each couple hugs while a happy Father Bede raises his own hands—clapping—and tells the congregation, "Now let's give them all the clap!" Dante and Abigail exchange a look of surprise. They try—unsuccessfully—to suppress giggles. Both know it's time to leave quickly, before the couples' recessional blocks their getaway.

"Oh, what a dear man. I hope he never learns what giving someone the clap means," Dante says with a laugh, buckling his seat belt. "Someday, I'd like to tell him about how valuable his penance was—because it led me to you. Unfortunately, this wasn't the time."

"Not while he's giving the clap," Abigail says.

Dante and Abigail's outdoor wedding at the Selby Gardens was a treat for a small group of friends and loved ones after the long confinement. Episcopal Bishop Billings came to marry them. Nick was Dante's best man and Benaiah stood up for Abigail; Joan and Vera read the Epistle and the Psalm. Chairs were socially distanced, so a mic was necessary even for their small group. Harold and his St. Francis Gardens neighbors sat in a section marked with the American flag. On the other side of the lawn, Liberty Garcia, Paul, and Jake Bisignano sat, watching Barry and Cecilia try to keep the twins happily occupied. No one cared if the little ones became restless, but at the exchange of vows, Cecilia got up to walk behind those seated, jiggling Ana, as Barry sat Andres on his lap. All were grateful for a beautiful day, with no threat of rain.

Harold & Maggie

Harold was used to keeping a busy schedule and getting plenty of exercise on his bike, even at age seventy-four. But he began to feel overly tired, even on days when he hadn't done much. Then night sweats reappeared—he thought he was done with that. It was the swollen lymph nodes that took him to the VA doctor, who quickly recognized Hodgkin's lymphoma. Not uncommon for Vietnam vets exposed to Agent Orange.

His St. Francis neighbors pitched in—delivering his groceries and medicine, keeping him company when he needed it. Dante began to worry: how long might it be before Harold wouldn't be able to live alone?

Then suddenly Harold got the astonishing news that his long-ago wife—Maggie—was coming, after all these years. In her older age, Maggie had begun thinking back to her time with Harold, doubting he was still alive, but wondering. Her computer-savvy grandson said he'd find out. It didn't take long for him to inform her that a Vietnam Veteran named Harold Johnson lived—alone—in Florida. "But I found three 'Nam veterans named Harold Johnson'," he warned her. "The only other thing I know about the Florida one is that he keeps bees and talks about them to kids at a nature preserve."

"That's my Harold!" Maggie cried. "Alive and well!"

She felt great relief, along with renewed guilt. *Was there something I could have done?* She wondered. The Harold who came home from Nam scared her. She didn't know what to do. And there was no help then. Those vets were scorned, returning in such terrible shape—lost even to themselves. *But somehow he got well! He may no longer be the Harold I knew, but neither one of us is our teenage self.*

I'm going to see him!

Her grandson directed her to the St. Francis Gardens website, and Maggie texted Benaiah Jones, saying that she and Harold married as teenagers, then divorced after he came home from Vietnam. After forty-eight years, she'd like to see him again and wonders if there's anything she should know before attempting to contact him. Asking for any advice Benaiah found pertinent to give, Maggie hit "Send."

Intrigued, Benaiah forwarded the email to Abigail, who—equally intrigued—forwarded it to Dante. All agreed that this offered an exciting possibility of brightening Harold's days now. Abigail replied, saying she'd be happy to discuss Maggie's visit with Harold—and her hunch was that he would be willing and eager. She closed by saying that after she talked to Harold she would call Maggie to discuss a visit. Abigail knew that Maggie would also need to know about Harold's lymphoma. But that discussion was premature now.

###

Maggie's coming! A delighted Harold got a barber to make a house call. Outside, the barber shaved his beard and gave him the buzz cut he had when they married. A stark new look from olden days, so much so that on the evenings that Harold and Maggie sat outdoors, his neighbors saw a cleanly shaven man they hardly recognized talking to an attractive woman whose face looked too young for her white hair. The neighbors heard a lot of laughter. Sometimes they noticed a slight tremor in Maggie's hand when she lifted a bottle of water to drink.

Harold was seeing only the "Magpie" of their youth. He reminded her that he'd given her that old nickname because magpies are the most intelligent animals in the world—and also the rare bird that can recognize itself in a mirror.

"But I was sixteen!" she said, laughing. "Teenage girls were absorbed with our looks then—hair to shoes. I avoid mirrors now!" Harold would hear none of it. "You haven't changed a bit," he claimed, "I'd have known you anywhere."

He saw only the girl he'd married. That beautiful smile. The sky-blue eyes. The same regal posture. She'd always worn gemstone colors—ruby, emerald, sapphire—and still looked stunning in them.

Maggie was with Harold when he died, four months later. Abigail conducted the funeral Mass and offered prayers at his burial at Sarasota National Cemetery. After "Taps" was played, the flag was given to Maggie.

Abigail and Dante asked Maggie to speak after his Burial of the Dead Service that evening. Wearing an aquamarine linen dress and sensible shoes, Maggie walked to the pulpit. Her hand shook as she unfolded a paper on which she'd written notes so she wouldn't forget all she wanted to say. She lifted her reading glasses held by a chain around her neck to put them on, but looked over them at her new friends to begin:

"I'm Maggie. I grew up with Harold in Hermann, Missouri. Our town was so little it only had two Yellow Pages, back in the day. We were eighteen and nineteen when we married. He was drafted, and the Harold I'd married didn't return from Vietnam—as you all know. I didn't know what to do to help him or how to cope. We divorced, and he left town.

"I eventually married again and spent the rest of my life in Kansas City. I was widowed ten years ago. In the past few years, I've wondered if Harold was still alive— knowing the odds are that he wasn't. You think often of the past late in life when you're no longer mired in work deadlines and kids. And, in 2020, stuck indoors with not much to do, I wondered about Harold even more often. It was a blessing to be reunited after all this time.

"A first love remains forever in memory; its indelible moments return even more frequently in old age. We started dating when I was sixteen. I recalled Harold knowing all the words to what was then an old song of our parents' era: "Autumn Leaves." Every fall he'd sing to me:

The falling leaves drift by my window
The falling leaves of red and gold
I see your face/Those summer kisses
The sunburned hands I used to hold.

"He knew all the verses—though it was written as if an older person were recalling a love, now gone. Much of my life—living in Missouri with four distinct seasons—in the autumn I'd recall Harold's unusual teenage sensitivity to that song.

"I have happy memories of Harold's first car. He had to work year-round on the farm and had to earn enough to buy it himself. It was so old he gave it an old man's name: Oscar. Its radio had only two buttons: City and Country. It didn't have turn signals—so Harold had to stick his arm out the window—rain or snow—when he needed to turn. With Oscar, our parents didn't have to drive us anymore on dates. For us as teenagers Oscar was Freedom!

"In those snail-mail days, we wrote letters when we were apart during summer vacations and his Vietnam stint. I kept his letters all these years in an old metal box. Somehow I knew—even when we were teenagers—that Harold was beyond his years in seeing many things—and people—more clearly than you'd expect in a boy then.

"Harold's dad abandoned his family when Harold was seven. By middle school, Harold was the first kid I knew living with a stepdad. Divorce was rare in that time and place, especially among Catholics. By junior year, a second kid of divorce moved to town and this kid was getting into trouble. I said to Harold that maybe that was because of that kid's parents' divorce. And Harold said, 'Well, yeah, that's tough. But, at some point, you have to just get on with your life.' That was Harold at seventeen. Even then, it struck me as a mature take on surviving tough times and the importance of having a good life. Something none of the rest of us had needed to learn so young.

"These memories led me to look for him. And I learned that you folks had rescued him and stuck by him while he went through detox and therapy. Got him a home of his own. Where he was working with his beloved bees. I found the Harold I'd known and loved.

"When he first saw me, he threw out his arms and said, 'Darling Magpie, welcome.' That nickname goes all the way back. As we caught up, Harold didn't spare me details of the life he'd had out on the streets. Then his gratitude when he told of Dante, looking him in the eye when they talked. Passersby don't usually look street people in the eye. Dante asked questions. Listened to him. Laughed with him. By the grace of God, Dante saw, during their first brief meeting, the Harold I'd loved.

"And, well, you folks knew Harold, so you won't mind if I quote him. Harold told me, 'All those years on the streets were hell. At best—I only got hind titty. Convinced that's as much as street people deserve. Getting off the streets put me through purgatory—those counselors were kickin' ass and takin' names. But there's *hope* in purgatory. Those counselors also had my back. We made it through to this— our houses, neighbors, the bees, and the Nature Preserve. Heaven right here on earth!'

"The soldiers at the cemetery gave me the flag. But I found Harold late in life and was privileged to help care for him in his final months. There's a better place for this flag. Many of you know the Tiny Homes headquarters office is moving to a new building. Other cities throughout the state and country are asking for help and direction to do what you've done here. So an outreach program will soon be launched.

"Harold was the first resident—who welcomed all the others. You called him the Mayor of St. Francis Gardens. The new outreach building is where Harold's flag belongs, as the program expands to serve other veterans throughout America.

"You neighbors, Dante, and the Reverend Abigail, and Benaiah Jones, and all you Sarasota Veterans brought Harold back to his love of life. Obviously, you loved him too. I thank you."

Benaiah returned to Miami from the funeral. Abigail had recommended her to Bishop Billings, advising him that she needs a staff of three to begin expansion of the project to the Southeastern Coast and central Florida. Other congregations in other states are now getting interested. Abigail's vision and Dante's good deed survive in unforeseen ways after Harold's death: it extends beyond tiny houses.

It shows America's traumatized and marginalized Veterans that they matter. The boomerang effect of giving these Veterans a hand up is that they're encouraged to help others. Adding a good deed to one life has resulted in a multiplication of good intentions and actions as everyone involved considers how to do good to improve the world.

19

Magnetic Paint/2059

Dante was wrong to believe at age fifty that he'd already lived more than half of his life. He lived to be one hundred and one. Centenarians are common now. Dante liked to remind people that three Supreme Court Justices are centenarians—all appointed back in the days of President Trump.

Dante lived to see his four great-grandchildren provided by the twins—Ana and Andres.

Before that, he and Abigail made yearly trips to Ontario back when Ana played as a catcher on Canada's Women's National Baseball team. She went on to manage the Chicago Cubs.

Andres conducted the Baltimore Symphony Orchestra and continues to play cello in semi-retirement, in Baltimore and abroad. Another daughter—Joan's "Little Sister" Vera—is an education specialist at Mote Laboratory & Aquarium, facilitating the translation and transference of scientific information to a global audience.

After getting his MD from Northwestern, Jacob Bisignano became an intensivist physician, spending his workdays solely in the ICU attending to the needs of critically ill patients.

Dante enjoyed the memory of giving his father-of-the-bride toast at Joan's wedding. At age fifty-seven, Joan married Parker Coleman, her "little sister" Vera's one-time teacher. He and Joan had kept in touch for the first couple of years after Parker moved to Georgia for a coaching job.

A year later, Joan learned on Facebook that he'd married. It wasn't a surprise.

She hadn't known that he was widowed two years ago until he called her one day. After a brief long-distance romance, Parker retired and moved back to Sarasota and bought an Ace Hardware store. Cecilia, Vera, and Malena were the happy bridesmaids at their wedding. Dante spoke about Joan's first meeting with Parker, some twenty years earlier.

"In those days, she always checked out a person's feet and shoes. So she took note of Parker's size sixteen feet right away—actually, it's sixteen on the left foot and size fifteen on his right! Everyone's feet are slightly different, but when they get that big it can sometimes require two sizes. She wears a size twelve on both feet. From the very first meeting, it was obvious that these two share a mutual 'good understanding'." His daughters groaned, and everyone laughed.

It was lighthearted fun then, as Dante didn't want to get into what he'd learned in time—that it's a blessing to recall a first love fondly as you vow "til death do us part" to a second love. You usually don't realize the first time that even a good marriage will end badly, with one spouse's death. Death seems so far away then, it's as if you're talking about another lifetime. And if you're lucky, you are.

You later learn that every leap of love requires hope alongside an awareness of eventual heartbreak. But consider the even sadder alternative of never leaping toward love. He was pleased that all his girls finally took that leap. Cecilia and her daughter Ana and Joan and Vera.

The men they brought into the family enriched his life, too.

Dante loves Abigail's reply when people ask how they met: "I went into Ace looking for magnetic paint, and we got attracted to each other." *Hard to believe we've been married thirty-seven years. Time goes by so quickly now.*

He thinks of the tiny house project—*growing beyond anything imagined when we built those first dozen homes. Changing the lives of thousands of Veterans—who then go on to help others.* His New Year's resolution was to cherish all the best moments of his life, *having so many keeps me busy enough.*

Now at the end of the year, Dante has weakened. Sometimes he calls Abigail Lilliana. That's OK with Abigail. Some mornings she'll greet him with: "I'm Abigail. Do you know me?" and he always says yes. She has begun to suspect he isn't sure. In the last few weeks, Dante sometimes thinks he's in an Ace store. When anyone comes into the room where he is, he'll often ask, "May I help you with anything?"

Whenever it's Abigail—as it usually is—she'll reply: "I'm looking for magnetic paint." Then going over to his bed or chair to hold his hand, she'll say, "But I'm drawn to you," and kiss him. He laughs as if it's the first time he's ever heard it.

She was holding his hand at his bedside when he died.

"May I help you?" were Dante Moretti's last words.

Photo Credit: Charles Fara Photography

Carol DeChant has published in Chicago's *Tribune* and *Sun Times*, and the Miami *Herald*. Her non-fiction books include *Momma's Enchanted Supper* and *Fifty Great American Catholic Eulogies*. The latter won First Place in the Independent Book Publishers Association's Audio Book of the Year contest. *Are You Free* is her first novel. She lives in Sarasota, FL.

Check out her website to learn more about Carol: www.caroldechant.com

Acknowledgement

When I began this novella as my 2020 New Year's Resolution, I knew my story would stretch from 2008 into 2020 and beyond. I had no idea a pandemic was coming. As that soon became clear, I froze for two weeks: how could I possibly get my characters to do all they needed to do, masked, socially distanced, and mostly home alone? Of course, we all learned to do everything we had to do then, as did my characters.

Those whose own lives—including a few Confession stories—I've drawn upon and/or tweaked include David Ashby, Amanda Bernier, Angel Berardi, Matt Bernier, Margot Gessler, Karla Libbey, SaraJane Patten, and Michael Theodore. The inspiration for the character of Abigail is Frances Kemble—who built her own tiny house and does her own wiring.

Real-life counterparts in the professions of some characters also contributed to this book.

These include nutritionist Julie Bender-Sibbio; Therapist Robert Bakst, both Sarasotans; the Reverend Paige Hanks of St. Petersburg; and Louis W. Robin, bug sniffing dog trainer par excellence, working in Mesa, AZ.

One character has her real-life counterpart's actual name: Bernadette DiPino was Sarasota Chief of Police during the time of this novel; she told me what she would have told the protagonist to do in their scene.

Father Mario Saragana is a fictional priest, echoing something often heard at Sarasota's St. Martha Catholic Church in that time: to pray for the one who broke your heart.

Jim Alberti, RIP, originally from Sicily, owned the Main Street Barber Shop. That scene is total fiction.

The Tampa Bay Rays appear as they struggled and prevailed, providing excitement and hope to locked-in fans after the delayed 2020 MLB opening. Their amazing season, culminating in triumph over the astronomically overpaid Yankees and the 2019 cheating Astros in the Playoffs, gave hope to my characters—as well as to real-life fans in our eight months of pandemic confinement.

My priest-character Abigail cites the work of Dr. Robert Sapolsky, a bioneurologist at Stanford University; her professor was inspired by Dr. Abraham Joshua Hescehel's work *Moral Grandeur and Spiritual Audacity,* Susannah Heschel, editor.

This work could not be in your hands without the expertise of novelists Joan Dempsey (*This Is How It Begins*), Vinita Hampton Wright (*Dwelling Places*), and Cathy Pezdertz (*Being Lili*). Input from fellow writers was essential to the work's progress. They are Meredith Ashby, Esther Cohen, Jack Dierks, Grier Ferguson, Harriett Harrow, Kelly Hughes, Barbara Lanctot, and LaVonne Neff.